"Tell me somethi...

"Are you marrie...

Sean cleared his throat, an uneasy expression crossing his face. "Uh, no." He took a step back. "I'd, uh, better be going now. You have a lot to take care of. You probably can't return the wedding dress, but maybe your guests will let you keep the gifts—once they realize this isn't your fault...."

"What size jacket do you wear?" Laurel quickly turned and retrieved a garment bag from a hook on the back of the standing mirror. "I'm pretty sure this will fit," she murmured as she unzipped the bag and glanced down at his shoes. She could still salvage something from this mess. "I doubt we'd be so lucky that the shoes would fit, too. Edward had really big feet."

"No way. I'm not getting all dressed up so *I* can tell your guests that you're not getting married," Sean said. "I've done what I came here to do. I'm leaving."

"I don't want you to tell the guests," Laurel said. "I do plan to get married this afternoon."

"Eddie is in jail. And I don't think they'll let him out."

"Oh, I'm not going to marry Edward," she said. "I'm going to marry *you*."

Dear Reader,

I can't believe that the last episode in my MIGHTY QUINNS saga is finished and in your hands! When I started this project, I signed on for three books. And now, seven books later, I've married off all the Quinns—Conor, Dylan, Brendan, Keely, Liam, Brian and finally, Sean.

It's no wonder Sean was the last to find love. He's been the one to resist it more than any other Quinn. But when I chose Laurel Rand as the heroine of this book, I knew that Sean was a marked man. No matter how hard he tried, love was going to get him. He was about to fall very fast and very hard.

I hope you enjoy the last book in my MIGHTY QUINNS series. I can't tell you if I'll write any more. I'm sure there are Quinn cousins out there somewhere, waiting to find love. But for now, you can visit www.katehoffmann.com to learn more about my upcoming releases for Harlequin Books.

Happy reading,

Kate Hoffmann

Books by Kate Hoffmann

THE MIGHTY QUINNS miniseries

Kate Hoffmann
The Mighty Quinns: Sean

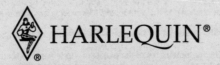

HARLEQUIN®

TORONTO • NEW YORK • LONDON
AMSTERDAM • PARIS • SYDNEY • HAMBURG
STOCKHOLM • ATHENS • TOKYO • MILAN • MADRID
PRAGUE • WARSAW • BUDAPEST • AUCKLAND

To old friends and new fun.

To Mary, Jane Y., Lisa, Lori,
Jan, Ruthie, Susie and Jane W.

ISBN 0-373-69141-6

THE MIGHTY QUINNS: SEAN

_____Prologue_____

SEAN QUINN sat on the front steps of his house on Kilgore Street, his chin cupped in his hand, his elbow resting on his knee. He didn't have to look down the street to know his twin brother, Brian, was approaching. But right now, he didn't want to talk to Brian. He didn't want to talk to anyone. He just wanted to be left alone.

"Sean!"

"Go to hell!" he shouted as Brian strode up the front sidewalk.

"Come on, don't be that way. Why didn't you stick around? She wanted to talk to you. You just stood there like a lump."

Sean's fists clenched and he fought the impulse to strike out, to put a nice purple bruise on that pretty face of Brian Quinn's. "She wanted to talk to _you_," Sean shouted. "She's only pretending to like me so she can get to you. I'm not stupid. I see the way she watches you."

Brian stopped cold, his jaw agape. A frown wrinkled his brow. Sean took a small amount of satisfaction that he'd had the rare opportunity to best his brother. When it came to the mysterious motivations of seventh-grade girls, Brian still couldn't tell when he was being hosed.

Sean unclenched his fists, knowing that he couldn't hit his brother for simple stupidity. Still, he wouldn't mind popping Brian good just for fun. Although they were twins, they didn't have much in common beyond looks. Brian was part of the cool crowd at school, always knowing how to act and what to say. The teachers loved him, the girls adored him and he had a wide circle of buddies who seemed to hang on his every word.

Sean was known for nothing more than the fact that he was Brian Quinn's brother—the shy one, the dumb one, the silent one. He'd always struggled to fit in, knowing Brian's friends expected so much more from him—and were constantly disappointed when he didn't deliver. When Colleen Kiley started paying attention to him, he thought, for one brief instant, that he might have found someone who actually saw him for who he was. But it hadn't taken him long to realize what she was really after. He had always been able to sense when he was being manipulated or lied to.

"She...she doesn't like me," Brian stuttered. "She told me she likes you."

"Get real. Sometimes you can be as dumb as a pile of dirt," he muttered as he turned and walked to the front door. "Go ask her to the dance and see if she doesn't say yes. She doesn't want to go with me, she wants to go with you. She's just using me to get to you."

Sean yanked open the ragged screen door and stalked inside, letting the door slam behind him. He stormed through the house, past his little brother Liam, who was sprawled on the floor watching television, and past his oldest brother Conor, who had just come home from the police academy. Dylan, a high school senior, was off with one of his friends and Brendan was sitting quietly at the kitchen table, his nose buried in some dumb book about India.

Life was relatively normal, now that their father, Seamus Quinn, had left for another swordfishing run on the *Mighty Quinn*. They'd be without their only parent for at least another month, but Sean almost wished his father wouldn't bother coming home at all. His infrequent periods of residence only threw the family into turmoil and emphasized the fact that the six Quinn brothers were existing on the edge, just a few steps ahead of the social workers and the bill collectors, just a few dollars away from eating ketchup soup for dinner.

Conor had managed pretty well over the years and kept the family from falling apart. Now that he'd graduated from high school and was bringing home a regular paycheck, the future looked a little brighter. Their father's luck at poker no longer determined whether or not they'd go to bed with empty bellies.

Sean hurried to his bedroom and closed the door behind him. After flopping down on his bed, he covered his eyes with his arm. Sometimes his twin brother was so dense. Jaysus, for a guy who had so many girls drooling over him, he should have figured them out a long time ago.

Each of the Quinn boys had a particular quality they were known for. Nineteen-year-old Conor was the steady one, the provider. Dylan, the next oldest, was the playboy. All he had to do was crook his finger and every girl within a hundred yards was his. Then there was Brendan, the dreamer. He was fifteen and already he could tell the best stories, better than any of the Mighty Quinn tales their father told.

And Brian. For a thirteen-year-old, Brian was smart. He got the best grades in school, he'd been elected class president and he was good at sports. He could stand up in front of the class and give a report without turning all red and fumbling over his words. Sean could already tell that, someday, Brian would be famous. Maybe he'd even be on television. His youngest brother, Liam, was only ten, so Sean wasn't sure what he'd be good at.

But Sean wasn't good at anything. With a soft groan, he rolled over and hung off the side of his bed. He pulled a shoebox from the bottom drawer of the bedside table, then sat cross-legged on the bed and set it in front of him on the tattered quilt. He pushed off the lid, then flipped through the contents—his stamp collection, his baseball cards, a purple rabbit's foot—until he found the small framed picture of the Virgin Mary.

Sean knew his brothers snooped through his treasures, but he also knew that none of them would even consider pinching his picture of the Blessed Virgin. Whether it was superstition, fear of eternal damnation or just a lack of interest in religion, Sean didn't care. The important thing was that the framed picture made a perfect hiding place.

He carefully pulled the easel back off the picture and withdrew a faded photo he'd hidden there eight years ago. He'd managed to keep the photo a secret, from his brothers and his father, all these years. Maybe that was his talent, Sean mused as he stared at the only surviving photo of his mother—he knew when to keep his mouth shut.

He'd been just three years old when Fiona Quinn had walked out of their lives. His father's anger and sadness had cast a gloom over the house and he'd begun to drink heavily and gamble more than usual. Two years later, Seamus told them their mother had died in a car crash. All traces of her had been wiped from the house. Though his brothers had grieved for a time, they had quickly moved on.

But Sean remembered. He remembered the spot, now empty, in front of the stove where she used to stand. And her smell—he remembered that she always wore perfume and a red apron. When he'd found the photo, caught behind a kitchen drawer, he'd tucked it away, preserving the only evidence he had of Fiona Quinn's existence.

He rubbed his thumb gently over her face, as if he were touching her. She was the prettiest lady he'd ever seen. She had beautiful shiny hair and twinkling eyes. And a smile that made him feel better just to look at it. And she was kind and understanding. She was his angel, and whether she was dead or alive, he still felt her presence.

"Ma," he murmured. He closed his eyes and tried to imagine her saying his name. In some secret corner of his mind, before memories even began, he found the sound and it was soft and calming, making the anger he held so tightly inside of him dissolve.

A knock sounded at the door. Sean scrambled to return the photo to its hiding place. When he'd shoved the box back into the drawer, he laid down on the bed.

"I don't want to talk to you!" he shouted, knowing it would be Brian. His brother hated it when people were mad at him.

"It's my room, too," Brian replied. He knocked again, more insistent.

Sean hopped up and unlocked the door, then flopped back down on the bed. "You don't have to be such a pest."

"I can come in if I want. You can't keep me out of my own room."

"Suit yourself," Sean muttered. "But I don't have to talk to you."

Brian sat on the end of Sean's bed and crossed his arms over his chest. "You know, you shouldn't be mad. After all, you are a Mighty Quinn. We all know Mighty Quinns aren't supposed to like girls. Da says they're dangerous. Falling in love with girls will destroy us. Just suck the strength right out of us."

Sean laughed derisively. He'd heard the Mighty Quinn stories for as long as he could remember and recognized them for what they were. "Yeah, well, if you believe all that crap Da feeds us, then you're dumber than *two* piles of dirt."

The stories had become a part of their family history, stories of strong and clever and brave Quinn ancestors who had slain dragons and fought ogres and rescued fair maidens. Though he'd enjoyed the tales when he was younger, he soon saw them for what they were— elaborate lies, filled with his father's hidden warnings about the evils of the opposite sex.

"Remember that story about our long-ago cousin Ronan Quinn?" Brian slid a little closer.

"I don't want to hear a story," Sean insisted.

But Brian wouldn't be deterred. He loved the stories. "Ronan was from a poor family who lived in a little cottage at the edge of a huge forest. His father was always away and his mother struggled to feed a family of six. When the last potato was eaten and the last bit of flour gone, Ronan knew they were in a desperate state."

"I don't want to hear a damn story!" Sean insisted.

"Yes, you do," Brian said. "It will make you feel better."

"So he decided to take his club and dagger and go deep into the woods to hunt the wolf," a hesitant voice continued. Sean and Brian glanced over at the door to see Liam peeking in, adding his own part of the story. He waited, expectantly, hopefully, and when Brian nodded, Liam raced into the room and threw himself on the bed between them.

Brian reached out and ruffled Liam's dark hair. "If Sean won't have a story, then I'll tell it to you."

Liam grinned. "I love this story."

Sean cursed beneath his breath and slouched on the bed, determined not to listen to another ridiculous tale of imaginary ancestors.

"The king had put a bounty on the head of every wolf in Ireland," Brian continued, "and the bounty was enough to feed Ronan and his family for many years. But hunting wolves was a dangerous sport, especially for one so young. And with only a wooden club and a small dagger, Ronan would have to come face-to-face with a wolf in order to kill it—close enough to be killed himself."

"Wolves have really sharp teeth," Liam commented. "My teacher showed us a picture of one. They can kill a man."

"Now, Ronan had never gone to the dark forest and wasn't sure how to find the wolves. But he vowed to stay in the woods until he found his prey and killed it—or was killed himself. Hunger and thirst tormented him from the start. Then he came upon a small quail with colorful green and yellow feathers and thought, *Here is my dinner.* But just as he was about to kill the quail with his dagger, the bird turned to him and spoke."

Liam spoke up in a high, wavering voice, "'Please,' she begged Ronan, 'spare my life and if you do, I will give you a magic acorn. The acorn will give you one wish, and I will give you a piece of advice.'"

Brian nodded. "That's right. And Ronan, always tenderhearted, couldn't bring himself to kill the quail. So he took the acorn and bent closer for the bird's advice. And what was it?"

"'These woods are full of magic,'" Liam said.

"So Ronan wished to have a bucketful of money, but nothing happened. 'I've made a bad deal,' Ronan said to himself as he headed deeper into the woods. He'd been fooled and all he had was a silly acorn in his pocket. Hours later, he still hadn't seen a wolf or found a bite to eat. But he came upon a huge black boar, rooting in a clearing near a beautiful crystal stream. Ronan's stomach growled and again he thought, *Here is my dinner.* He snuck up behind the boar and raised his club, but the boar turned and spoke. 'If you will let me live, I will give you a magic acorn and a bit of advice,' the boar said. But Ronan wasn't about to be duped again. He wasn't that stupid."

"Yes, he was," Liam said. "He took the acorn even though he was starving. And he got more advice. 'Everything is not as it appears in the magic forest.' That's what the boar said. And that was good advice. Wait and see."

Sean groaned. "Do we have to? You both know how the story ends. Ronan meets the deer with antlers of gold and gets a third magic acorn and more advice. 'What you want and what you need are not always the same.' And then he meets a wolf and—"

"No," Brian interrupted. "This version is different."

"How?" Sean demanded.

"Ronan meets a...a beautiful druid princess dressed in...in a sparkling white gown, with a crown of emeralds covering her long, blond hair. Ronan had never seen a woman so beautiful and he was immediately captivated."

Liam frowned. "Wait. That's not how the story goes!"

"Yes, it is," Brian insisted, shushing his brother. "The druid princess saw that he possessed three magic acorns and, with three, he could have anything he wanted. She desired them for herself. So she bewitched Ronan and told him that she could offer him anything he wanted for each of the acorns. When she offered to trade him one of his magic acorns for a wonderful feast, Ronan quickly agreed. The moment she took the acorn, a delicious feast appeared before his eyes. Ronan tossed his dagger aside, for what would he need a dagger for if he had such food to eat? He reached for a shank of beef. But before he was allowed to touch the food, the princess offered him something more. A bow appeared, made of the finest silver, and a jeweled quiver full of arrows. Ronan gave her another acorn and quickly tossed his club away, for he could now hunt wolves with his new bow and arrows. But before he could touch the bow and quiver, the princess offered him one final trade. His last acorn for a beautiful steed with a fine leather saddle."

"Hey! Didn't you hear me calling?" Conor stood at the door, dressed in his Boston Police Department T-shirt and navy trousers. His hands were braced on his waist and, for a moment, Sean was taken by how different he looked—older, like a real adult. He wasn't just his pain-in-the-ass big brother anymore. In a few months, he'd be a cop. "Dinner is ready. Come on, it's getting cold."

He disappeared and Liam turned back to Brian. "Finish the story. It's just fishsticks and French fries."

Brian turned to Sean. "Do you want me to finish?"

"You might as well," Sean said, knowing that Liam would refuse to leave until he heard how the Mighty Quinn triumphed in the end.

"When Ronan saw the fine steed, he thought, *I will catch many wolves with such a fine horse and I will collect many bounties and make my family rich.* He pulled the last acorn from his pocket. But then Ronan hesitated. The acorns must have very powerful magic to be so valuable to the princess. The druid princess demanded the third acorn, her voice turning shrill and her face turning ugly with anger. Ronan suddenly remembered the advice he was given by the quail, the boar and the deer."

"The woods are full of magic, everything is not as it appears and what you want and what you need are not always the same," Liam repeated.

"'No!' Ronan cried, clutching the last acorn in his fist. In the blink of an eye, the feast, the quiver and bow and the fine horse disappeared, for they were an illusion. And the princess turned into a huge, vicious wolf, snarling and lunging toward him, trying to get him to drop the acorn. Ronan had thrown aside all his weapons and had no escape."

Even Sean wasn't sure how the story would end, for this was a completely different version of Ronan's tale from the one his father often told. In his father's tale, the wolf guarded a princess and Ronan killed the wolf and rescued the princess. Then he chastely returned her to her father and went on his way, because Mighty Quinns never fell in love.

Brian paused and waited, dragging out the moment.

"All right, what happened?" Sean finally asked.

"Well, Ronan gathered his courage, held the single acorn tightly in his fist and closed his eyes, wishing that the wolf would turn into a harmless animal, like a mouse or a rabbit. When the snarling and growling finally ceased, Ronan opened his eyes and in front of him was a beautiful golden wolf pelt, worth a fine bounty from the king. He carefully lifted it up and, to his surprise, an ugly toad jumped out. When the druid princess realized a magic acorn had been used to turn her into a toad, she hopped off into the woods, and Ronan headed for home, anxious to collect his bounty.

And after that, there was always food on Ronan's table.''

Sean couldn't help but laugh at the tale's ending. ''That story doesn't even make sense. If Ronan was so smart, why didn't he just go home with the acorns and wish for something he really needed? And what did a princess need with magic acorns if she had a crown of emeralds? And if she had two acorns already, and Ronan had one, then she could have—''

''Aw, shut yer gob,'' Brian said, giving him a shove. ''It's just a story. Who's gonna believe in magic acorns anyway?''

''It was a good story,'' Liam said, his voice full of appreciation. He scrambled off the bed. ''And I know the moral. Never trust a woman, no matter how pretty she is. A Mighty Quinn can never fall in love.'' He ran to the bedroom door, then turned back. ''Oh, yeah, and don't get too greedy when someone offers you really nice stuff.'' He ran out, shouting to Conor that he was starving.

Brian stood and Sean followed his lead. He did feel a little bit better. To hell with Colleen Kiley. Brian could have her, and good riddance. Besides, she really wasn't even that pretty. She had squinty eyes and she wore too much makeup, and when she laughed, she sounded like a hyena.

''One more thing,'' Brian said as they walked out of the bedroom.

''If you're going to ask if I'm taking Colleen Kiley to the dance you might as well say goodbye to your pretty teeth right now,'' Sean said, '''cause I'm gonna knock them through the back of your head.''

Brian laughed. Then he held out his hand. "I thought you might be able to use these." He dropped three acorns into Sean's palm.

"What are these for?" Sean asked.

"I figured you could use them to turn Colleen Kiley into a toad. Or maybe a big old sewer rat." Brian pulled three more out of his pocket. "And if that's not enough, I've got three of my own to use." He slipped his arm around Sean's shoulders. "We Quinns gotta stick together, right?"

Sean smiled and nodded. No matter how much he fought with his brothers, he always knew he could depend on them. "Yeah, I guess we do," he murmured, shoving the acorns into his pocket.

1

SEAN QUINN sat slumped in the front seat of his battered Ford sedan. He'd found a parking space right down the street from the three-flat located in one of Cambridge's trendy neighborhoods, and he'd been watching the front door for almost two hours.

The case had come to him in a roundabout way, through a colleague he'd met while sitting in a bar one night. Bert Hinshaw was a hard-drinking, woman-chasing, sixty-year-old private investigator, a guy who had seen his share of crazy cases over the years. They had talked for hours, Sean learning from Bert's experience and Bert grateful to have someone to listen to his tales. A friendship developed and they now met regularly to chat—Bert doing most of the talking and Sean taking mental notes.

But health problems had slowed Bert down, and every now and then he threw a case Sean's way. Sean had been on this referral for nearly two weeks, hired by a wealthy woman who had been romanced, married, then bilked out of a fortune by Eddie "The Cruiser" Perkins aka Edward Naughton Smyth aka Eddie the Weasel and about six or seven other aliases.

This case had been by far the most lucrative he'd ever taken, even better than the Intertel Bank case he'd had a few months ago. He was making some real money, a guaranteed rate of nearly four hundred dollars a day.

Eddie, a notorious con man and bigamist, had left a trail of broken hearts and empty bank accounts across the country. The FBI had been after him for years. A bail bondsman from Maryland had been on his tail since Eddie had jumped bail in Baltimore. But Sean had been the one to track him down when Eddie's seventh wife had heard that he was in the Boston area. She had hired Sean to find him and to turn him over to the FBI, so she might exact her own retribution at a trial.

Sean glanced at his watch. On Saturdays, Eddie usually didn't get out of bed before three in the afternoon. And last night had been a late one. He'd spent the evening with one of his five current lady friends, a wealthy divorcée with a Bentley and a pricey house in Back Bay. Sean had decided that the time was right to move in and had called the FBI. The agent in charge had assured Sean that he'd have two men to the flat within the hour.

"Come on, come on," he murmured, staring out at the sideview mirror for a nondescript sedan.

It amazed him that a guy like Eddie could convince nine intelligent women from across the country to marry him and then entrust their money to him. He had to admire a guy that smooth. Not that Sean had any problems attracting women. He was a Quinn and there was something in the genes that made the Quinn brothers irresistible to the opposite sex. But, unlike his brothers, he'd never had an easy time talking to women. He just couldn't think of anything witty or charming to say, nothing to keep them amused—beyond his talents in the bedroom.

Things hadn't changed a whole lot since he was a kid. Brian was still the outgoing twin and Sean stood in the background—observing, evaluating. His brothers teased him that his aloofness was exactly what made him irresistible to women. The less interest he showed, the more fascinated they became.

But he knew what all those girls really wanted— great sex and a future he wasn't prepared to give them. He recognized their need to own him, to trap him into marriage, and he always made his escape before he got caught. Quinns weren't supposed to fall in love. And though that no longer applied to his five brothers, Sean had no intention of making the same mistakes they had.

A gray four-door sedan slowly cruised past his car and he sat up. "It's about time," he muttered.

He stepped out of the car and a few seconds later two agents, dressed in dark suits and sporting government-issue sunglasses, approached. "You Quinn?" one of them asked. "I'm Randolph. This is Atkins. FBI."

"What took you so long? Did you have to stop for doughnuts?" Sean muttered.

"We were out catching some real bad guys," Atkins said, his disdain apparent.

Sean held up his hands in mock surrender. "If you're not interested, I can call the bail bondsman. He'll come up from Baltimore, they'll haul Eddie back there. Your Baltimore guys can have the collar."

Sean knew the uneasy relationship between the Feds and bounty hunters. If they could make the arrest without too much bother, they preferred to take it rather than risk the embarrassment of being outwitted by amateurs. Either way, Sean was in for a nice finder's fee from the bail bondsman. He wasn't about to give that up.

"So what apartment is he in?" Atkins asked.

Sean gestured to the building. "He's a creature of habit. On Saturdays, he leaves at precisely 3:00 p.m. Gets a cappuccino at the coffee shop down the street, buys the *Racing News* at the newsstand, calls his bookie on a pay phone. A little shopping, dinner around seven, then he heads out for the night."

"How long have you been watching this guy?"

"Two weeks," Sean said, his gaze returning to the front door of the building. He watched the door open and couldn't help but smile when Eddie stepped out—right on schedule—dressed in a tailored sport coat and perfectly pressed trousers. Though he was in his mid-forties, Eddie made a point to stay in shape. He could easily pass for a man ten years younger. He carried a leather overnight bag, an ominous sign for a guy like Eddie. Was he preparing to run? "That's him," Sean murmured.

Atkins looked at his watch. "Two fifty-five. I guess you don't know your guy as well as you thought you did." He stepped into the street and Randolph followed. "We'll take him. You stay here."

"The hell I will," Sean muttered. "If he bolts, I want to be close enough to catch him."

They were halfway across the street when Eddie saw them. Sean knew before the agents did that he was going to run. Sean could see it in that split second when their eyes met. It was that knowledge that gave him a jump on the agents. Before they could even shout, Sean took off after Eddie. He caught up to him halfway down the block, grabbing him around the waist and wrestling him to the ground.

By the time Randolph and Atkins reached them both, Sean had Eddie pinned, his hands twisted behind his back. Atkins cuffed Eddie, then yanked him to his feet. "There are a whole bunch of ladies anxious to see you again, Eddie," the agent said.

"Wait, wait," Eddie said. "You can't take me now!"

Randolph laughed. "You want us to come back later? Yeah, right, we'll do that. In fact, why don't you just call us when you're ready to turn yourself in?" He shoved Eddie toward the car, but Eddie stopped and turned back to Sean.

"Hey! Hey, buddy!" he shouted. "Come here."

Sean glanced at the two agents and they both shrugged. "What do you want?" he asked.

"You gotta help me out. It's really important." He tried to reach into his pants' pocket, but the agents grabbed him. Atkins pulled out a wad of bills secured in a fancy money clip. "Give the guy fifty," Eddie said. "No, make it one hundred."

The agent handed Sean two fifties. "What's this for?" Sean asked.

"I want you to go over to 634 Milholme Street and tell Laurel Rand what happened."

"You'll get a phone call," Sean said. "You call her." He pushed the money back at him.

"No, I can't. By then it will be too late. You gotta do

this for me. Tell her I'm real sorry. Tell her I really loved her."

Sean stared down at the money. He should refuse, but every dollar in his pocket was one more dollar toward a real office and maybe even a real secretary. One hundred dollars would pay the electric bill for a few months. Why not take a few minutes and run a simple errand? "All right. You want me to tell her you were arrested?"

Eddie nodded.

"You want me to tell her why?"

"You might as well. Once she learns the truth, she isn't going to want to talk to me again. But tell her I really did love her. She was the one."

"Yeah, Eddie," Agent Randolph muttered. "I'm sure that's what you tell all the ladies. Do you say that before or after you pick their bank accounts clean?"

"I loved them all," Eddie said. "I just have this compulsion. I keep asking them and they keep saying yes. That's their fault, not mine!"

"Let's go." Agent Randolph dragged Eddie away by the arm.

"Remember, you promised," Eddie shouted at Sean. "I'm counting on you."

The agents pushed Eddie into the back of the sedan, then roared off down the street. Sean glanced at his watch again. It wouldn't take him more than a half hour to deliver the message. After that, he'd head back to his apartment, type out a final invoice and get it in the mail. By next week, he could have his money, and the week after that, he could start looking for a small office. There was still advertising and office equipment to think about, of course. And he'd need a phone and an answering service and a beeper. If he was going to build a successful business, he'd have to start dressing for success, too—like suits and maybe a tie or two.

He strolled over to his car. "Milholme Street," he murmured. "This should be fun."

Milholme was only a few miles from Eddie's place. Sean squinted against the midday sun, pulling his sunglasses down to read the numbers on the homes along the wide boulevard. But when he reached the address Eddie had given him, he discovered it wasn't an apartment or a business, but a church.

He pulled the car into a spot on the street. Parked near the front of the church was a long limo with a Just Married sign pasted to the back. "What the hell is this?" Suddenly he regretted saying yes to Eddie. The last thing he wanted to was to tell some woman that she was going to be dateless for the wedding festivities.

Sean noticed several single women standing in front of the church, dressed in their Saturday-afternoon finery. One of them had to be Laurel Rand. He jogged across the street and approached the first woman he met. "I'm looking for Laurel Rand," he said.

"She's inside," the pretty guest replied.

Sean nodded, then took the steps two at a time. The sooner he took care of this responsibility, the sooner he could get over to Quinn's Pub and celebrate the successful closing of a case. He found a bridesmaid just inside the doors, clutching a bouquet of flowers in her hands. "Laurel Rand?" he asked.

"She's down that hallway," the bridesmaid said,

pointing to the left. "Last door on the right. Are you the photographer?"

Sean frowned at the girl before he headed down the hall. He wasn't sure what to expect when he knocked on the door. But when a woman dressed in a bridal gown opened it, he knew taking the money from Eddie had been a colossal mistake. He'd just been thrown to the lions and he was wearing sirloin shorts. "Laurel Rand?"

"Yes?"

Sean swallowed hard as her gaze met his. He recognized her as one of the women he'd seen with Eddie over the past few weeks. But he'd never realized how beautiful she was. She looked like a angel, all pale and perfect, dressed in white. He had to clench his fingers just to keep from reaching out and touching her. Her wavy blond hair was pulled back from her face and tucked beneath a veil, but a tiny strand had slipped loose, the only distraction from absolute perfection.

Her dress rustled, startling him back to reality. "You're Laurel Rand?" Sean repeated, all the time praying that Laurel Rand was somewhere else inside the room, maybe arranging the flowers or polishing the bride's shoes.

"Yes," she said. "Are you the photographer? You were supposed to be here an hour before the wedding." She reached out and grabbed his hand, then pulled him into the room. Her touch was warm and caused an unbidden reaction. "We only have thirty minutes before the ceremony is supposed to begin. How are we going to get all the shots I wanted? Where is your equipment?"

"I—I'm not the photographer."

She let go of his hand. "Who are you? And why are you interrupting me? Can't you see I'm the bride? You're not supposed to make me nervous," she babbled. "I'm supposed to be calm. Don't I look calm?"

He fought the temptation to grab her hand again, to hold on tight while he gave her the news. "You...you look—" Sean took a deep breath, searching for a word to adequately describe her. "Beautiful. Stunning. Actually...I'd say...breathtaking." For a guy who had trouble talking to women, he certainly wasn't having any trouble now.

A tiny smile curled the corners of her mouth. "Thank you."

Sean wanted to turn and run, content to keep the memory of Laurel Rand in his head just as she was when she smiled. To hell with Eddie. He was a bigamist, nine times over. But still, some inborn instinct to protect her from humiliation kicked in. "Can we talk?" he asked, reaching out to take her by the elbow, anxious for any excuse to touch her again.

"Talk?"

He shut the door, then gently steered her toward a chair, just in case she decided to faint. "Who are you marrying today?"

She stared at him for a long moment with a confused expression. "I—I'm marrying Edward Garland Wilson. But you should know that, if you received an invitation to the wedding." Her brow furrowed slightly. "Are you crashing my wedding? Who are you?"

"Just one more question," Sean said. "Is your groom about six-one, dark hair, graying at the temples?"

"Yes," Laurel said. "Are you a friend of Edward?"

"Not exactly. But he did send me here to give you a message," Sean said.

Her expression brightened. "He did? Oh, that's very sweet. But he could have come himself. I don't care about those silly superstitions about seeing the bride before the ceremony. What's the message?"

Sean cursed silently. Jeez, why had he agreed to do this? He should just turn around and get the hell out of Dodge. He didn't need to break this woman's heart. And he certainly didn't want to see her cry. But he suspected there was no way he'd get out of the room without doing both.

He took a deep breath and gathered his resolve. "Edward won't be coming to the wedding."

LAUREL STARED at the handsome stranger, unable to comprehend what he was saying. "Is this some stupid joke?" she asked. Sure, it might be fun to tease the bride on her wedding day, but this was downright cruel. Didn't she have enough to worry about?

"I'm afraid it isn't," the man replied. "Eddie gave me a hundred dollars to come over and tell you personally."

"No," Laurel said, shaking her head, panic quickly setting in. "This can't be happening. I have to get married today. There are guests and bridesmaids. I spent two months picking out the music. He cannot get cold feet thirty minutes before we walk down the aisle!" Laurel pushed past the stranger. "Where is he? I want to talk to him." She cursed beneath her breath as she headed to the door. They had an agreement! And he wasn't allowed to back out, especially at the last minute.

He grabbed her hand as she brushed past him, his touch firm and sure. "He's not here. And you can't talk to him."

"Why not?" she demanded as she yanked out of his grasp.

"Because he's on his way to jail," he said.

Laurel spun around and faced him. "Who are you? And why are you here?"

"I told you. Eddie sent me. My name is Sean Quinn. I'm a private investigator. And I'm..." He paused. "I'm the one who sent your groom to jail."

She gasped. "Jail? You sent Edward to jail?" She wasn't sure what possessed her at the moment. Maybe it was all the stress of the last few months—planning the wedding, making sure everything was perfect, finally finding a suitable man who wanted to marry her. Laurel didn't expect a fairy-tale wedding, but she didn't expect this nightmare, either! She balled her fingers into a fist, cursed beneath her breath, and punched Sean Quinn squarely in the stomach.

The punch caught him by surprise and the air left his lungs in a loud whoosh. For a moment he didn't breathe. He just looked at her with shock. Then he took a ragged breath. "Nice punch," he said. "I—I guess I deserved that." He slowly straightened. "But I expected a few tears, not a right jab." He cleared his throat. "I think after I explain, you might feel a little better."

She leveled a withering gaze at him. "The only thing that will make me feel better, Mr. Quinn, is if you disappear into thin air and Edward appears in your place."

"That's not going to happen. Your fiancé isn't who he pretends to be. His real name is Eddie 'The Cruiser' Perkins. He's a con man and he's wanted in eight states."

"You must be mistaken. Edward is from a very good family in West Palm Beach. They're in international banking and investments. I met his parents."

"They were probably actors he hired," Sean said. "That's his modus operandi, according to his sheet. He's very good at what he does. You shouldn't feel bad for being duped."

"Duped?" Laurel said.

Sean Quinn gave her a weak smile. "I—I didn't mean duped. I—I'm not saying that you're stupid."

"Stupid?" She felt an edge of hysteria creep into her voice and she fought the urge to punch him again. "You think I'm stupid?"

"No," Sean countered. "Not at all. I think you're—"

"Naive? Trusting? Gullible?"

He shook his head and swallowed hard. "Like I said before. Beautiful."

His gaze met hers and for a moment she couldn't breathe. He had the most amazing eyes, an odd mixture of gold and green, strangely intriguing, yet direct, honest. Since he'd walked into the room, she hadn't really bothered to take a good look at him. After all, this was her wedding day. She was supposed to have her mind on her groom.

Frustration welled up inside of her and she felt like screaming. This wasn't the way things were supposed to go. This wasn't the most romantic day of her life, but it did represent a milestone of sorts. From this day on, she was supposed to be in control of her life.

Laurel walked over to the window and fixed her gaze on the courtyard outside. "The best laid plans..." she murmured. How could they have gone wrong? "I can't believe this is happening."

"I'm sorry," Sean said, placing his hand on her shoulder. "I—I really didn't mean to mess up your special day."

All of a sudden, exhaustion overwhelmed her. She turned back to Sean. "It's all right. It's not your fault." A tear dribbled down her cheek and she angrily brushed it away. All this planning and now...nothing.

"Hey, don't cry," he murmured. He gently rubbed her arms, as if to soothe her. But the moment he wrapped his arms around her, all thoughts of Edward and her ruined wedding fled from her mind. Instead, Laurel was taken by his kindness and his strength...and his incredibly muscular chest.

She sucked in a sharp breath, then stepped back. If she had any questions about the depth of her feelings for Edward, they were answered now. She hadn't loved him. He was out of her life barely ten minutes and she was in the arms of another man!

Laurel walked across the room, determined to observe Sean Quinn from a safe distance. His eyes weren't the only part of him that she found attractive. His hair was dark, almost black, and brushed the collar of his leather jacket. He was handsome, but there was something else, an air of indifference about him that made him seem aloof, untouchable.

"What was he arrested for?" Laurel asked.

Sean cleared his throat. "Ah...bigamy."

Laurel gasped. "Bigamy? He has a wife already?"

"Actually, he has nine. You'd have been number ten."

Laurel groaned, a flush of humiliation warming her face. "I guess this is what I deserve." She smiled weakly. "I should have suspected something was up. I wanted him to meet my friends, but he always had some excuse, some business meeting that he had to attend. And when I asked about his family, he changed the subject. And then he couldn't make the wedding rehearsal last night. He said he had a business meeting."

"He was with another woman," Sean said. "But if it makes you feel better, he said he really did love you."

Laurel laughed. Love. She was far too practical to believe in that particular emotion. She and Edward were compatible, and she'd thought he came from a good family, so she'd decided to accept his proposal when he'd asked. After all, it had fit right in with her own plans. She would marry Edward, collect her trust fund from her uncle, and make all her dreams come true. And now, everything was ruined.

Or was it?

"Tell me something," Laurel said, lifting her gaze to Sean and sending him a smile. "Are you married?"

He shook his head. "No."

"Do you have a girlfriend or a fiancée?"

He cleared his throat, an uneasy expression crossing his face. "I better be going now. You have a lot to take care of. You probably can't return the wedding dress, but maybe your guests will let you keep the gifts—once they realize this wasn't really your fault."

"What size jacket do you wear?" Laurel quickly turned and retrieved a garment bag from a hook on the back of the standing mirror. "I'm pretty sure this will fit," she murmured as she unzipped the bag and glanced down at his shoes. She could still salvage something from this mess. "I doubt if we'd be so lucky that the shoes would fit, too. Edward had really big feet."

"No way. I'm not getting all dressed up so I can tell your guests you're not getting married," Sean said. "I've done what I came here to do. I'm leaving."

"I don't want you to tell the guests," Laurel said. "I do plan to get married this afternoon."

"Eddie is in jail. I don't think they're going to let him out," Sean replied.

"Oh, I'm not going to marry Edward. I'm going to marry you."

Laurel waited, the silence in the room deafening. His jaw slowly dropped and he stared at her as if she'd just sprouted horns and a tail. Maybe the suggestion was a little rash, but she was desperate. "Before you say no," she murmured, "I want you to listen to my proposal."

He backed away from her, his hands up. "I don't need you to propose, lady. I'm not walking down the aisle. Not with you, not with any woman."

"And I have no intention of calling off my wedding. Now, as I see it, this is entirely your fault. You're the one responsible for Edward getting arrested and—"

"He was a damn bigamist!" Sean shouted. "He was

breaking the law. And you should be grateful I saved you from him."

"I would be, if there wasn't so much riding on this wedding. There are guests and gifts and a huge reception planned. The embarrassment would be..." She let her words drift off. She felt a bit guilty for manipulating him, but the wedding *was* important. Once she got married, she'd get her inheritance. Once she got her inheritance, she could rent her building. She had it all picked out, an old brick storefront with lots of light and high ceilings.

The idea had come to her several years ago when she'd started teaching music at a grade school in Dorchester. After college, she'd bounced around from job to job, trying to find her place in the world. She'd joined the Peace Corps on a whim, only to find herself with a chronic case of dysentery. They'd sent her home after four months. A few months later she'd taken a job teaching dance on a cruise ship. But the exotic locales didn't make up for the cramped quarters and the seasickness. Her career as a flight attendant ended when she'd realized she had a paralyzing fear of flying.

But this time she'd found something she might actually be good at. There were plenty of after-school programs for kids who were interested in academics or athletics, but very few available for children with talent in the arts. So she had decided that once she got her hands on her five-million-dollar trust fund, she'd open an after-school center that focused on theater and dance and music, and maybe even the visual arts. She already had a picture of it in her mind. And she would call it the Louise Carpenter Rand Center for the Arts, after her mother, who had passed down her love of the arts to Laurel.

If her uncle Sinclair hadn't been such a miser, she might not have had to go to such extremes. But he controlled the Rand family trust, doling out money as he saw fit. And since he'd been named the administrator of her trust fund after both her parents had died, he held the purse strings. Sinclair had laid out the conditions. The trust fund provided her with a small monthly income. If she married before her twenty-sixth birthday, she would be entitled to her inheritance of five million. If she remained single, she'd have to wait until her thirty-first birthday for the money.

In truth, Sinclair Rand was nothing more than an old chauvinist. In his mind, no woman could handle that amount of money without a man to supervise. He hadn't cared who she married, he hadn't even bothered to meet Edward. As long as her husband had a penis, then Uncle Sinclair figured he had the brains to handle her finances, and that was enough for him. Uncle Sinclair claimed his ideas were in keeping with how Laurel's father, Stewart Rand, would have wanted things. But she also knew if her parents were alive, they'd support her idea for the arts center.

But two could play at her uncle's little game. "You mentioned you were a private investigator. I suppose you're accustomed to being paid for your time. I'm willing to pay you ten thousand dollars to put on this tuxedo and walk down the aisle with me."

He gasped. "Ten thousand dollars? You're crazy."

"I'm not asking you to marry me. It wouldn't be legal. We don't have a marriage license. All I'm asking is that you walk through the ceremony with me." She paused. "And the reception. You just have to pretend to be Edward. Think of it as playacting. And once we're in the limo and on our way to the honeymoon, that's it. Your part is over."

It would be a way of buying herself some time, Laurel mused. Sooner or later her uncle would have to see that his insistence on marriage was antiquated and untenable. After all, she'd nearly married a criminal to get her hands on her inheritance. Pretending to marry a handsome private investigator wasn't nearly so serious. Once her uncle saw how far she was willing to go to build her dream, he'd have to relent.

"All this just to save you a little embarrassment?" Sean asked, leveling her with a suspicious gaze.

"Yes," she lied. He didn't really need to know the truth, did he? After all, she was paying him well for his services as a stand-in groom.

"And you're going to pay me to do this?"

"Yes. Ten thousand. That's a lot of money," she said. "You could afford to get a decent haircut."

He stared at her for a long moment, his gaze intense. "I'm not sure I trust you."

She felt a shiver skitter along her spine. She'd planned a wonderful honeymoon in Hawaii and was tempted to make that a requirement, as well. Maybe another ten thousand would cover a week of frolicking on a secluded beach. An image of Sean Quinn, shirtless, his skin burnished by the sun, flitted through her mind. It was immediately replaced by an image of him diving into the surf...naked...the water gleaming over his—

Laurel cursed inwardly. This was getting ridiculous! She'd nearly married another man today and she couldn't stop fantasizing about a guy she barely knew. "I'm not paying you to trust me. I'm paying you to marry me. If it will make you feel better, I'll put it all in writing."

He thought about the offer for a moment longer, then sighed. "All right. I suppose I could help out. I could use the money."

Laurel threw herself into his arms, unable to contain her joy and relief. But when he slipped his hands around her waist and held her just a bit longer than proper, she found herself wondering what it might feel like to kiss Sean Quinn. "I—I'll write out our agreement while you get ready." She hurried to the door, then turned around before she opened it. "You're not going to back out on this, are you?"

Sean picked up the tuxedo and looked at it critically. "With that right jab you've got? I'd be fool to make you angry again."

THE DOOR CLOSED softly behind her. Sean released a tightly held breath, then shook his head. "What the hell am I doing? I've got to be insane." He glanced over at the window and wondered if he could get it open and crawl out before she returned.

The day had started out with such promise. He was going to close a big case, take a sleazebag off the street and collect a nice fat fee. But he'd made an error in judgment by offering to do a favor for that sleazebag and look where it got him. He hadn't needed Eddie's hundred-dollar fee; he'd already had a good day financially. Greed had gotten him in this mess.

He thought back to the tale of Ronan Quinn, how the wolf had nearly eaten him because he'd gotten a little too greedy. Now he had a chance to collect a tidy ten thousand acorns from Laurel Rand, just for pretending to be Edward Garland Wilson.

It would be ten hours' work maximum, at a rate of one thousand dollars an hour. He'd have to be a fool to turn that down. And what did he have to lose? His only real plans this evening had been to stop by Quinn's Pub and have a few beers, then go back to his apartment and type up the bill. And Laurel Rand was right—he hadn't signed any marriage license, so the whole thing was off the books. Just a charade for her high-society wedding guests.

Sean slowly unzipped the garment bag and withdrew the tuxedo. He checked the label, noting the fancy designer name. The jacket looked like it might be a little small and the pants on the short side, but at least the shirt collar wouldn't choke him.

This was certainly not what he had in mind when he thought of marriage. Of course, he'd never thought of marriage for himself at all. Sean had been told all the cautionary tales of his Mighty Quinn ancestors—as had his brothers. But Sean had been the only one in the family to recognize that the odds were against all six brothers being able to achieve eternal bachelorhood. When his oldest brothers had fallen victim, he had assumed that his odds for avoiding matrimony had improved considerably.

But there was a part of him that envied his five

brothers—and even his little sister, Keely. They'd all found something that he'd never once experienced in his life. Sure, there had been women, even a few who imagined themselves in love with him. But not one had come close to touching his heart—a heart that he'd kept well protected over the years.

His attitude about marriage might not have been so harsh had he a decent example to follow. His father had been horrible at it. And his mother had been... Sean paused. He used to think of her as an angel, the perfect mother. But that had changed one day, shortly after his fourteenth birthday, when he'd learned the truth about his parents' marriage.

He shook his head, pushing the thoughts aside. His father's imperfections and his mother's infidelities were in the past—so why couldn't he forget them? A shrink might say he had trust issues, but Sean didn't believe in that kind of psychobabble. He was who he was and there was no use trying to analyze it. He just had to live with it.

Sean took a deep breath, shrugging out of his jacket and dropping it over the back of a chair. Then he stripped down to his boxers and tugged on the finely pressed black trousers. He'd just pulled the zipper up when the door opened.

Laurel Rand slipped inside and hurriedly closed the door behind her, turning to face him. For a moment she froze, staring at him mutely, her gaze dropping to his naked chest, then flitting back up to his face. His eyes met hers and for a moment he was struck again by her beauty. But then he forced himself to look at her rationally. She'd just learned her groom wouldn't be attending the wedding, yet she'd seemed to accept the news without hysterics and tantrums.

Sean rubbed his hand over his abdomen, his muscles still tense from when she had punched him. Every instinct told him that Laurel Rand shouldn't be trusted, but the money was just too good to resist. Ten thousand dollars didn't fall into his lap every day. "Yeah," he murmured. "I'll do it."

A tiny smile curled her lips and Sean took satisfaction in the knowledge that what he was doing had pleased her. She really was extraordinarily beautiful, especially when she smiled. Some might think her mouth a little too wide or her cheekbones too high. Taken alone, each feature of her face wasn't all that pretty. But when put together, she had a beauty that he found arresting.

She slowly approached and handed him a folded piece of paper. "I wrote it all out," she said. "And...and I wrote you a check. It's dated for the day after tomorrow."

He took the paper and the check, then grabbed the tuxedo jacket and put them both into the breast pocket. "Thanks."

"Aren't you going to read it?" Laurel asked.

He shrugged as he slipped into the pleated shirt. "I trust you." Sean stared down at the front of the shirt. "No buttons," he said.

"Oh, there are studs," she said, grabbing up the garment bag and fishing around until she found a card. "Here."

Sean fumbled to get one off the card, but his fingers were clumsy with nerves. It dropped to the floor and skidded beneath the chair. "I never could figure these things out," he said, bending to retrieve the stud.

"Let me," Laurel said, taking the errant stud from his fingers.

He stood in front of her, the shirt gaping open. When her fingers brushed his skin, a current of sensation rushed through him. He held his breath as she worked at the studs, trying to focus his thoughts on something other than a vivid fantasy of her smoothing her palms over his naked skin and brushing away the shirt altogether. Of her damp lips trailing across his—

She glanced up at him and Sean sent her a weak smile.

"Do they fit?" she asked.

"They?"

She sank down, picked up one of the black patent leather shoes, and held it out. Sean slipped it on his left foot and found it had to be two sizes too big. "They'll be all right."

"No," she said. To his surprise, she reached down the front of her dress and came back with a wad of tissues. "Here. Stuff some into the toes." She pulled out more tissue and tossed it over her shoulder. "I didn't need the cleavage anyway."

He bit back a chuckle. Her honesty was disarming. "Aren't you nervous?" he asked.

"Why would I be nervous?"

"Aren't all brides supposed to be nervous?"

She ran her hand over the front of his pleated shirt. "I'm not getting married today," she said. "You saw to that."

A trace of anger colored her voice and he immediately felt regret for his part in her distress. "I'm sorry," Sean said. "But I think it's for the best." He paused. "Did you love him a lot?"

Her hand stilled on his chest and she fixed her gaze on the shiny pink paint on her fingernails. "I obviously didn't know him," she said in a resigned tone. Laurel forced a smile. "I suppose we should talk about what's going to happen. You have been to a wedding before, haven't you?"

"Quite a few lately," Sean said, thinking of his married siblings.

"Good, then you know how it works. You'll go up to the front of the church and wait for me at the altar."

"Do I have a best man?"

"No," Laurel said. "Edward phoned me last night to tell me his brother, Lawrence, couldn't make it. He had a family emergency, something about his pregnant wife. But then, that might have been a lie. He probably doesn't even have a brother." She reached for his tuxedo jacket, then held it out for him. "It's a traditional service. Short and simple. Just listen to the minister and repeat everything he tells you to."

"I can do that," Sean said, turning away from her.

She slipped his jacket over his arms, then smoothed her hands across his shoulders. "That's not such a bad fit," she said. "I need to go get my bouquet and to talk to the photographer, so I guess I'll see you at the altar."

Sean slowly turned back to face her. "Are you sure you want to do this?"

Laurel nodded, then started for the door. But she stopped before she opened it. "One more thing," she said. "Can you act as if this is the happiest day of your life?"

"I can try," he said.

She slipped out of the room. Sean grabbed the shoes and stuffed a wad of tissue in each of the toes. He found socks in the garment bag and quickly pulled them on before slipping into the shoes. He wanted to make this work for her. He wasn't sure why. He only knew that she was in trouble and she'd asked for his help.

And there was something about her that drew him. He didn't have to measure every word he said with Laurel. She'd been bluntly honest with him, told him what she needed and how she felt. He hated the games that went on between men and women, the coy looks and the subtle innuendo, the advance and retreat meant to lead to the bedroom. His brothers were good at the game, but Sean always felt as if someone hadn't shown him the rule book.

Laurel Rand didn't play games. When she didn't like what he had to say, she punched him in the stomach; when she needed his help, she simply offered to pay him for it. She hadn't tried to manipulate him into something he didn't want to do. He had to admire a woman like that.

When he finished tying his shoes, he made an attempt at the bow tie, but each time, it turned out lopsided. After the fifth try, he decided to settle for crooked. He raked his hands through his tousled hair, then stared at his reflection. He didn't look too bad. "This has got to be the strangest day of your life, boyo," he muttered before turning and walking to the door.

He walked down the hall. In the distance, he saw Laurel standing in front of the entrance to the sanctuary. She turned and their eyes met for a moment. A hesitant smile touched her lips and Sean gave her a little wave. He stopped and held out his arms, then slowly turned so that she might approve of his appearance. She laughed, and then her three bridesmaids turned to look at him.

Sean pulled open the door and slowly walked up the side aisle of the sanctuary. He found the minister waiting for him in a small anteroom. "Well, we're almost ready to get started," the minister said. "Are you ready?"

"I guess," Sean murmured.

"I know you didn't have a chance to attend the rehearsal, but the service will be pretty straightforward. Just listen to me and I'll guide you through it. Any second thoughts?" he asked.

"What?"

"Marriage is for life, son," he said. "If you're not ready, then we don't have to walk out there."

"I'm ready," Sean said.

"Then let's go." The minister walked out the door and Sean had no choice but to follow him. He didn't have any idea what kind of sin he had just committed by lying to a minister. If he lied to a priest he'd be eternally damned, but the Episcopalians might be a bit more lenient on that point.

The minister stopped at the head of the center aisle. "You wait for your bride here," he whispered. "Then take her hand and come to the top of those three steps."

"Got it," Sean murmured. *Take her hand, then up the steps. Take her hand, then up the steps.* Though there was no reason for him to be nervous, he was. He didn't want to mess this up for Laurel. It seemed to mean so much to her.

Organ music suddenly filled the church and the doors opened. Slowly, bridesmaids dressed in pale green dresses marched down the aisle. When they'd arranged themselves in a line opposite Sean, the organ music swelled and Laurel appeared. Her veil obscured her face and even though he couldn't see her features, he'd never seen anything more breathtaking. For a moment Sean wondered if this was how a real groom was supposed to feel. But then reality intruded and he remembered that the next fifteen or twenty minutes would mean nothing at all. It was all just a charade.

When Laurel reached him, he took her hand and placed it in the crook of his arm. Together, they stepped in front of the minister. The ceremony passed without any major mistakes. Sean kept his eyes straight ahead until they had to exchange rings. He held her hand as he slipped the ring onto her finger and was surprised at how her hand trembled when she did the same. Yet he still couldn't bring himself to look into her eyes.

When the minister finally said, "I now pronounce you husband and wife," Sean breathed a silent sigh of relief. That hadn't been so hard. But the next command made his stop short. "You may kiss your bride."

Sean blinked and turned to him. "What?"

The minister leaned closer. "Lift her veil and kiss the bride," he said.

Sean looked at Laurel for her approval. Through the thin veil, he saw the tight smile on her face. "Kiss me," she murmured. "And you better make it good."

Sean didn't have to be told more than once. He took the bottom edge of her veil and lifted it over her head. Gently, he took her face between his hands and stared down into her wide eyes. Then, slowly, Sean brought his mouth down on hers. He had only meant to linger a few seconds—after all, this was a kiss meant purely for public enjoyment. He'd make it good. But the moment his lips touched hers, he couldn't seem to get enough.

He lost all perspective, forgot about the wedding guests watching them and the minister standing close by. Instead he focused all his attention on the sweet taste of her mouth, the way her lips parted hesitantly and the soft moan that slipped from her throat as he touched his tongue to hers.

Sean wasn't sure how long it lasted, only that when he finally pulled back, there was a polite round of applause from the wedding guests. "How was that?" he murmured, his mouth still hovering over hers.

"N-nice," she said in a shaky voice. Then the organ started playing and Sean, satisfied that he'd offered up his best effort, turned and held out his arm. As they started down the aisle, he glanced over at her to find her with the same stunned look on her face that he'd seen when he'd opened his eyes from the kiss.

Sean got the distinct impression that she'd enjoyed the moment as much as he had. Well, at least Laurel Rand was getting her money's worth. And if she wanted more, he would be happy to provide it.

2

THE RECEPTION WAS ELEGANT yet subdued, held at the Four Seasons, one of the city's most magnificent hotels. A small combo played dance tunes at one end of the room while guests relaxed at tables scattered around the dance floor. Laurel was quite pleased with how it had all turned out, after all the planning and the careful coordination. It had been a perfect wedding—except that the groom was in jail and she had "married" a stranger instead. But thankfully, no one had noticed anything amiss.

It was a wonder she had been able to get through the dinner at all. First there had been the toasts and then the obligatory kisses for the crowd. After their kiss in the church, Laurel didn't think it could get much better. But every time Sean's mouth touched hers, it was different, the sensations more acute, the taste of him more addictive. The last kiss they'd shared was on the dance floor and it had left Laurel dizzy and breathless and longing to drag him off into a dark corner.

She pressed her palm to her chest and took a deep breath. She just had to get past one more hurdle before the night could be called a success. Her uncle Sinclair would put in an appearance at the reception and she'd have the task of introducing him to Sean. Though Uncle Sinclair was over eighty, he was still as shrewd as he'd been when he and Laurel's father had made their first million together.

She looked out to the dance floor and watched as Sean swept one of her bridesmaids around. He hadn't been much of a dancer early on in the evening, but he had a natural athleticism that allowed him to pick up the steps with ease. And he didn't look bad in a tux, either. Any woman would be attracted to a man like...

Laurel frowned. Nan Salinger, her maid of honor and co-worker from West Elementary, looked like she was enjoying Sean just a bit too much. An unbidden surge of jealousy rushed over her and Laurel hitched up her skirt and headed to the dance floor. When she reached them, she tapped Nan on the shoulder. "I need to borrow my husband for a moment," she said. "It's time to cut the cake."

"Right," Sean said. "No problem." As if he were following orders, he immediately let go of Nan and walked off the dance floor toward the cake, leaving Nan alone with Laurel.

"I think you've found yourself a real prince," Nan said, staring after him with a dreamy gaze. "Why can't I find a man like that?"

"Like what?" Laurel asked, curious to hear what her girlfriend thought about her groom.

"Oh, I don't know. A manly man. You know, the strong, silent, sexy type. Broad shoulders, nice butt. He doesn't say much, does he? But that just makes him more intriguing. Does he have any single brothers at home? Because if he does, I want to meet them."

Laurel frowned. Nice butt? She didn't need to listen to this on her wedding day! "I—I don't know," she murmured. "I mean I'll let you know." She spun away, anxious to avoid more questions.

In truth, she didn't know anything at all about Sean's family...or Sean. She didn't know what he liked to eat or what he did in his spare time. She didn't know his favorite color or what kind of car he drove. And as she thought about everything she didn't know, Laurel realized that she'd never learn more. After tonight, Sean Quinn would walk out of her life and she'd never see him again.

"Miss Laurel?"

Laurel spun around to find her uncle's man, Alistair Winfield, trailing behind her. Her uncle never went anywhere without his man. Alistair served as butler, valet, personal chef and business manager to Sinclair. He also served as messenger boy. He'd been the one to tell Laurel that her reclusive uncle wouldn't attend the wedding ceremony. He'd been the one to sign the card with the wedding gift. And he'd made sure there was plenty of money in Laurel's checking account to pay for the wedding expenses.

"Hello, Alistair."

"You look very lovely tonight, Miss Laurel." The diminutive, balding man smiled warmly. "I'm truly sorry I wasn't able to see you walk down the aisle, but Mr. Sinclair had a very important meeting at the Numismatic Society. There was a discussion about a new Indian Princess pattern dime that was recently sold at auction."

As if her uncle didn't have enough money, he collected it, as well. He planned to leave all *his* money to the Numismatic Society of Greater New England. Laurel knew she could find better things to do with Sinclair's fortune than give it to a bunch of old guys who collected money, but that was his choice. She wanted to make her own choices about her inheritance, too. "Well, I'm glad he was able to make it to the reception," she said.

"He'd like to meet your new husband now."

"Where is Uncle Sinclair?" Laurel asked. "I didn't see him come in."

"He's waiting outside in the hall," Alistair said. "You know how he feels about crowds." He smiled weakly. "And women in strange hats. Plus if there are any flowers in the room, he'll demand that they be removed. You know about his fear of roses."

"I made sure to ask the florist to avoid roses," she said. "And we were just about to cut the cake, so as soon as we finish with that, I'll bring him a piece and introduce him to Edward."

"It's not chocolate cake, is it? Because you know how your uncle feels about chocolate."

Laurel winced. "I forgot about the chocolate. Sorry."

"Not to worry," Alistair said. "We'll be waiting. But only for seventeen minutes. Your uncle never waits more than seventeen minutes."

"I'll be there in five," Laurel said. She grabbed her skirt and hurried over to where Sean was waiting.

He stood with the knife clutched in his hand. "I have no idea how to cut this thing," he said, staring up at the four-tiered cake. "Should I start at the bottom or the top?" He glanced around the room. "Looks like we'll need about a hundred pieces."

"We only have to cut a piece for each other," Laurel

explained with a smile. "The photographer takes a few photos and then the caterer cuts the rest of the cake. I thought you said you've been to a wedding."

"I spent most of my time at the bar," he murmured. "They don't keep the cake at the bar."

Laurel grabbed the knife. "Put your hand over mine and smile," she said. The photographer snapped three photos before Laurel sliced into the cake. She took a small piece and held it up to him. "Here, eat this. And smile." He did as he was told. "And now, you feed me a little piece."

Sean frowned as he picked up a piece of cake and held it out to her. Laurel leaned closer and opened her mouth. But the moment her lips touched the cake, Sean let it go and most of the piece fell down the front of her dress. The small crowd that had gathered around the table laughed and clapped, urging Sean to retrieve the cake. He leaned closer and peered down her bodice.

"Don't you dare," Laurel muttered, her lips just inches from his ear.

Sean quickly stepped back and Laurel turned away from the guests to get the cake herself. When she'd restored her composure, she pasted a smile on her face and slipped her arm through Sean's. "Now, my uncle Sinclair is waiting to meet you. He's eighty years old, he's a little eccentric and he's going to ask you a lot of really weird questions. He'll probably want to see your fingernails. He has this thing about clean fingernails. Try to humor him as best you can, and if you don't know what to say, just squeeze my hand and I'll answer. Remember, your name is Edward Garland Wilson, you're from West Palm Beach, Florida, and your family is in international banking. Beyond that, he doesn't know anything about you."

"Why hasn't your uncle met Edward by now?" he asked as they strolled across the dance floor.

"Sinclair is a bit of a recluse. He lives in the Rand family summer home on Deer Island in Maine. He likes collecting coins and stamps and watching birds. He'll only eat green vegetables and he has seven pairs of shoes in exactly the same style and color. Oh, and he believes that aliens are living among us. But, please, don't get him started on that."

"He sounds a little crazy," Sean said.

"He's a multimillionaire," Laurel said, licking a bit of frosting off her finger, "so he's not crazy, he's eccentric." When they reached the door to the foyer, she took a deep breath. "Let's get this over with. After Uncle Sinclair, we can leave."

"And I was just starting to have fun," he said.

"Are you sure you can handle this with my uncle? If you don't think you can, then we can put it off."

"I'm fine," Sean replied. He slipped his hand around her waist and they stepped outside. Laurel longed for him to pull her into his arms and kiss her again, the way he had on the dance floor. But instead she forced herself to think about the task at hand, the final hurdle in her plan.

They found Sinclair Rand sitting silently in a small alcove just down the hall from the reception room, ensconced in a large wing chair like a member of the royal family. As they approached, he whispered something to Alistair and Alistair nodded. Laurel grabbed Sean's hand as it rested on her waist and gave it an encouraging squeeze. She could do this. She could turn this whole mess around and make something good of it.

"Hello, Uncle Sinclair," Laurel said, hanging on to Sean's arm like a lifeline. "Uncle, this is my new husband, Edward Garland Wilson. Edward, I'd like to introduce you to Sinclair Rand, my uncle."

On cue, Sean held out his hand. Sinclair took it, carefully examined Sean's fingertips, then let his hand drop. "You married my niece," Sinclair stated.

"Yes, I did," Sean replied.

The old man watched Sean from beneath bushy white eyebrows. "What do you eat for breakfast?" he asked.

At first, Sean seemed taken aback by the question, but then he jumped right in. "Cap'n Crunch. Sometimes I like Lucky Charms or Cocoa Puffs." He cleared his throat. "You look like an oatmeal guy."

Sinclair's eyebrow shot up. "I enjoy a nice bowl of oatmeal," he said in a gruff tone. "The old-fashioned kind, not the instant. Have you ever had any surgery?"

"No," Sean replied. "I'm a pretty healthy guy. How about you?"

"You know I have money," Sinclair continued, ignoring Sean's question.

"I have money, too. Probably not as much as you have. How much do you have?"

Laurel couldn't help but smile. Usually, people were intimidated by Sinclair Rand. But Sean seemed unfazed by the questions, turning them all back on her uncle with a directness that left her uncle off balance. "Uncle, we really have to go. Our honeymoon awaits. We're going to Hawaii."

"Hawaii? Don't eat the bananas there," he warned. "Stay away from all yellow fruit and you'll be fine. We'll discuss your inheritance when you get back."

Laurel bent down and gave her uncle a kiss on the cheek. "I'll call you when I—I mean, *we* get back." She gave Sean's arm a tug, but he stayed glued to his spot.

"It was a pleasure meeting you, Mr. Rand. I hope we'll have a chance to talk again."

Sinclair waved his hand as if to dismiss them both. Laurel decided it was best to make a quick exit before Sean said anything else. When they were out of earshot, she turned to him. "Why did you tell him that? You know you're not going to see him again."

"But he's not supposed to know that. In fact, if I was really Edward, I'd be expecting to see him again, wouldn't I?"

Laurel frowned. "Right," she murmured. "That sounds logical. Good thinking. Come on, we just have to say goodbye and I have to throw my bouquet. Then we're done here."

In truth, Laurel really didn't want the evening to end. Though her shoes were pinching and she'd be glad to get out of her dress, she really wasn't sure what she was going to do after this. She was due to leave for Hawaii early the next morning.

When she got back, she'd drive up to Maine and her uncle would present her with a check for five million. She'd lay low for a few months, then find a way to explain how the marriage had been a mistake. If she laid the blame on Sean—or "Edward"—then maybe her uncle might feel more sympathetic and understand her decision.

But even now, knowing what she knew about Sean, it was difficult to paint him as the horrible husband. Throughout this silly drama, he'd been so kind and supportive, and she'd begun to think of him as more than just a stranger collecting a fee for doing a job. For a brief moment in time he'd been the perfect husband—solid, dependable...and sexy.

She glanced over at him. Maybe she didn't know anything about Sean Quinn. But she did know how he made her feel when he kissed her and touched her. Wild and crazy and...breathless. And Laurel knew those were feelings she might never find again.

SEAN SAT IN THE BACK of the limo, his gaze fixed on the scenery as it passed by. The car had driven south out of Boston to Cohasset and now followed the shore through an exclusive neighborhood of old summer homes and beautiful mansions set near the water. Laurel had offered to drop him at the church first so he could retrieve his car, but he'd insisted that he could wait. He hadn't expected her to live halfway to Cape Cod.

Still, Sean was grateful for the quiet of the limo and a chance to spend a few more minutes with Laurel. Though she'd paid him for one day's work, he wasn't quite ready to call an end to their agreement. When he'd first accepted the check, he thought it might be a chore to go through the charade of a wedding. But the responsibility of spending the afternoon and evening with Laurel had turned from an unpleasant task into an enjoyable time.

He glanced over at her and found her absorbed in her own thoughts. "When does your plane leave?" he asked.

"Early tomorrow morning. I've got to be at the airport at 5:00 a.m. Uncle Sinclair is staying at the house, but I can sneak in, change and get my bags without waking him. The limo will drop you off back at your car. I'll drive myself to the airport." She turned to look at him. "What are you going to do for the rest of the night?"

"My family has a pub in Southie. Quinn's Pub. They're open until two. I'll probably stop there for a pint if it's not too late."

"I want to thank you for helping me out this afternoon," Laurel said.

"No problem," Sean said. Suddenly it had become so difficult to talk to her. He felt like the same old tongue-tied teenager rendered mute by a conversation with a pretty girl. "Hawaii should be nice this time of year." God, he'd sunk as low as the weather for a topic. It couldn't get much worse than that! Maybe he ought to cut his losses while he could and just shut up.

A few moments later the limo pulled into a wide circular drive, then parked in front of a huge stone mansion. "This is where I live," Laurel said.

"Jeez. It's huge."

"I know. It's too large for just one person. But the house was in the family, I grew up here, and Uncle Sinclair refuses to let me sell it, so I live here." Silence descended over them. "I guess this is it," Laurel murmured.

"I'll walk you inside," Sean offered. He pushed open his door and circled around the back of the limo, reaching Laurel just in time to help her out of the car. They walked hand in hand to the front door, her wide skirts rustling on the cobblestone driveway.

Laurel punched in the security code and the door automatically unlocked. She turned to him. "I guess *this* is it," she murmured.

"Not quite," Sean said. In one quick movement he reached down and scooped her up into his arms, then kicked the door open with his foot.

"What are you doing?" Laurel cried.

"Finishing the job," Sean muttered. He stepped inside the darkened house, then closed the door behind them.

"You don't have to maintain the charade for the limo driver. He doesn't work for the family. I don't think he's going to say anything."

If she thought he was playing a part for the driver, then she was sorely mistaken, Sean mused. He had just managed to come up with an excuse to touch her again and had taken action. Slowly, Sean set her back on her feet, but he let his hands rest on her waist.

He struggled with a sudden impulse, and lost. Throwing all caution to the wind, he kissed her, long and hard and deep. He needed to experience the taste and feel of her lips on his this one last time. Only then could he walk away.

What was it about Laurel Rand that he found so...comfortable? He'd fumbled with conversation for a moment in the limo, but the whole afternoon and evening he'd felt relaxed and easy with her. With other women, he'd always been on edge, unsure of what they wanted from him, suspicious of their motives. The deal he'd struck with Laurel had given him license to enjoy her without the usual games that came with romancing a woman. The instant he'd first touched her, and then when he'd kissed her, he hadn't been forced to think about what to do next. He'd just enjoyed the sensation.

Sean pulled back, but Laurel wrapped her arms around his neck and refused to let go. Slowly he backed her against the wall until her body was trapped against his. He pressed his hips into hers, surprised to find himself growing hard with desire. Where was his self-control? Why was it so simple to want her?

All those old tales of the Mighty Quinns raced through his brain but did nothing to stop him. His hands drifted up her rib cage at the same time his mouth traced a path down to her bare shoulder. If this had been a real wedding night, they'd be making love on the foyer floor before the hour was out. But they were not much more than strangers and this was a stolen moment.

"You should go," Laurel murmured as she furrowed her fingers through his hair.

"I should." He pressed his lips into the curve of her neck.

"We're going to be sorry if we let this go any further."

"We will," he replied.

She inhaled a ragged breath, then pressed her palms against his chest. "You're right."

Sean stared down into her eyes. "Sometimes I'm wrong." All she had to do was to give him the slightest sign and he'd carry her to the nearest bedroom. But he saw only indecision in her eyes. Why make this more complicated? He'd completed his end of their bargain and now it was time to walk away. Besides, he knew he was more suited to be her temporary bridegroom than her permanent lover. It was obvious that Laurel Rand was the marrying type—and he wasn't.

"It was nice being married to you," she whispered with a weak smile. "Thank you for helping me out."

"And thank you for the ten thousand," Sean said. He reached up and ran his fingertips along her cheek. "Have a good time on your honeymoon. I hope you find another husband—a *good* husband—soon. You deserve that."

Laurel nodded and Sean stepped toward the door. But the sound of her voice made him turn around. "Would you like to—" She paused.

"Would I like to what?"

A tiny frown furrowed her brow and then she shook her head. "Never mind. It was a silly idea. Goodbye, Sean Quinn."

"Goodbye, Laurel Rand."

QUINN'S PUB was crowded and noisy when Sean walked in. Saturday nights were always the busiest and now that Quinn's had been written up in a tourist guide as "authentically Irish," business had been booming. Sean hoped he'd find at least one brother in the bar, though with five of the six Quinn brothers now married or engaged, the odds weren't as good as they used to be.

Sean hadn't bothered to go home to change after he'd picked up his car at the church. On the ride over he'd been more preoccupied with thoughts of his short and very sweet "marriage" to Laurel Rand than his choice of wardrobe. There was a spot at the bar between two eager ladies and they smiled at him when he entered. Since the other brothers were off the market, the target on his back had grown much bigger. There was only one Quinn left and the girls who frequented the pub considered him the ultimate challenge.

But there was only one woman who occupied his thoughts tonight—his "bride," Laurel Rand. He strolled through the pub and was surprised to see his twin brother, Brian, behind the bar. His fiancée, Lily Gallagher, sat on a stool, deep in conversation with Brian. The three of them had lived together until the end of August when the newly engaged couple had found a new apartment.

A quick scan found Dylan and Meggie in the rear of the pub, playing pool. Lily saw Sean first and her expression was welcoming, but when Brian turned, he let out an astonished gasp. "What the hell are you wearing?" his brother asked.

"A tuxedo," Sean replied, sliding onto the stool beside Lily.

"I know it's a tuxedo, *eedjit*. Why are you wearing it?"

Sean shrugged. "I had an...event. You're not the

only one who can wear one of these things. I can be sophisticated."

"So what can I get you, Mr. Bond? A martini, shaken not stirred?"

"Give me a Guinness," Sean said. "And some duct tape for your mouth."

Brian chuckled as he grabbed a pint glass and wandered over to the Guinness tap. Sean slipped out of his jacket, then draped it over the bar. He withdrew a folded paper from the breast pocket and unfolded the agreement that Laurel had written out, his gaze dropping to the delicate scrawl of her signature. Suddenly the paper was snatched from his fingers.

"What's this?" Brian asked.

"Give me that," Sean said, standing to reach out across the bar.

"Brian, give it back," Lily insisted.

But his brother danced away. "Does this have to do with why you're dressed in that tux?" He stared down at the paper and began to read it out loud. "'I, Laurel Rand, promise to pay you, Sean Quinn, the sum of—' Holy shit. Ten thousand dollars?"

With a low curse, Sean braced his hands on the bar and jumped over it. He retrieved the paper from Brian's hand, then grabbed him by the front of his shirt. It had been like this their whole lives, the best of friends and then, a moment later, the worst of enemies. Maybe that's what twins were all about. "Stay out of my business," Sean said.

"What the hell is goin' on here?" Seamus demanded, wandering over to observe the commotion.

"Your sons are about to come to blows," Lily said.

"And I'm going to play pool with Dylan and Meggie before I get stuck in the middle." With a little wave, she headed to the back.

Seamus turned to Sean. "Get out from behind my bar. People will mistake this pub for some hoity-toity place if they catch a look at you."

Brian clapped Sean on the shoulder. "I didn't mean to get into your business."

"Yes, you did," Sean said.

"So why did you get all dressed up?"

Sean raked his hand through his hair. "Promise you won't say anything to the brothers?" They'd made the same promise hundreds of times before, a vow between twins who were closer than mere brothers could ever be. From the time Sean had broken the bedroom window and Brian had sworn to Conor that a bird had done it, to the time when Brian had snuck the keys for Dylan's car and taken it for a joyride. His secrets were safe with Brian.

"You know I won't," Brian said.

Sean leaned against the back bar. "I got married earlier this afternoon."

Brian's jaw dropped. He tried to say something, but words wouldn't come. When he finally regained his voice, he shook his head. "You got married? Just like that, without telling the family? I didn't know you were even dating someone. Hell, Sean, we've all accepted the fact that you're a little closemouthed, but this is taking it too far."

"It wasn't a real wedding," he explained.

"And that's just an imaginary tuxedo you're wearing?" Brian asked. He grabbed Sean's arm, dragged him down to the end of the bar, then flipped up the end section and shoved him through. "Go find us a booth," he muttered. "I'll get us something stronger to drink."

Sean found a spot near the front door of the pub, not exactly a quiet spot, but far enough away from prying ears to make conversation private. Brian joined him a few moments later with two shot glasses and a bottle of Irish whiskey. He set the bottle and glasses on the table, then slid into the seat across from Sean. Brian filled both glasses, snatched one up and downed it in one gulp. Sean did the same, then shoved the glass toward the bottle for another pour.

"Not until you tell me," Brian said.

"I've been tracking down a drifter named Eddie 'The Cruiser' Perkins. He romances wealthy women, marries them, then takes off with their money."

"What does he have to do with you getting married?"

"I found him and I was there when the FBI took him away. He asked me to do a favor for him. Gave me a hundred bucks to get a message to a woman named Laurel Rand. I didn't realize the address he gave me was for a church and that Laurel Rand was waiting there in her wedding dress. Waiting for Eddie. She didn't know he was Eddie the Cruiser, she thought he was Edward Garland something-or-other, her groom."

"So you just decided to marry her then and there? Isn't that taking your professional responsibilities a little too far?"

"She offered to pay me." Sean reached into his pants' pocket, withdrew the check and placed it on the table. "Ten thousand dollars to walk down the aisle with her. To pretend I was her groom for the rest of the afternoon and evening."

"But you married her," Sean said.

"Not for real. We didn't have a marriage license. I was pretending to be someone else. It's not legal. Hell, do you think I'd really marry a woman I just met?"

Brian grabbed the bottle and poured them both another shot. "Looking at it objectively, would you say you...rescued her?"

"Yeah," Sean said. "And then I married her. That's it. Don't you see? The curse is broken. I collect my money and it's over. No marriage, no curse. Clean and simple and safe."

Though the Mighty Quinn legends went back centuries, the Quinn family curse was a more recent development. It had begun the day Conor had met Olivia, and since then, every time a Quinn brother rescued a damsel in distress, he promptly fell in love with her. But that wouldn't happen to Sean. He'd neatly maneuvered himself around the curse.

"I don't think it's that simple," Brian said. "So when are you going to see her again?"

Sean looked down into his glass. "I'm not. I did what she asked, she paid me, and now I have enough money to rent an office and buy some office equipment. I won't have to operate my business out of the apartment anymore. Maybe I'll get a better class of clientele. Some corporate clients would be nice."

"I get the sense that you don't want it to end there."

Sean twirled the empty shot glass around in front him. "She was beautiful. I knew I shouldn't have gone along with her plan, that it was tempting fate. But I wanted to help her. And I'm glad I did."

"You know what I think? All those stories Da used to tell about the Mighty Quinns are just a load of crap. And so is this curse. There's a reason all of us fell in love with these women of ours. They were the right women in the right place at the right time."

"What does that have to do with Laurel Rand?"

"Maybe she's your perfect mate," Brian replied. "Maybe this is the right time and you just don't know it yet. Think about it. You've always kept your distance from the opposite sex. You didn't do that with this woman. Maybe there was a reason for that."

"That's a lot of maybes. You're in love and you're talking like a sap."

Brian sighed. "I'm simply saying that *maybe* you shouldn't write her off so soon. *Maybe* there's something there."

"Yeah, there's something there," Sean said as he slid out of the booth. He picked up Laurel's check and waved it at Brian. "Ten thousand and a chance to build my business. And that's all."

Sean waved goodbye to his father, then headed toward the door. He'd had a long day and the whiskey he'd downed was making him sleepy. But as he stepped out onto the street, Brian's words still rang in his mind. *Maybe. Maybe.*

When he reached his car, he slid inside and sat silently, his hands resting on the steering wheel. He couldn't deny he'd been thinking about his future more and more lately. He'd watched each of his brothers fall in love and find a happiness and contentment he'd never been able to imagine for himself.

It was a wonder any of them had found a normal life after their chaotic childhoods. Though he'd never been one to dwell on his choices in life, Sean had come to realize that his childhood had left more scars than he was willing to acknowledge. His feelings about romance and love, his insecurities about relationships and his mistrust of women all came from those formative days.

He deserved a happy future, but he wasn't sure it would happen for him. A niggling fear had been eating at his brain lately, an image of Sean Quinn, Private Investigator. Only he wasn't young anymore. He was old and worn out, looking like Bert Hinshaw, spending his days in a bar and his nights alone in a ratty apartment. Sean didn't want to see his future in that light, didn't want to believe life might pass him by.

How had his brothers found happiness? Had it really just fallen into their laps? Or had they gone looking for it? And once they'd found it, how had they known it was forever? These were questions Sean wanted to ask. But he'd been uneasy talking to his brothers about such subjects. It had been easier just to dismiss their relationships and to refuse to believe they'd last.

Sean knew where his own doubts came from. "Fiona," he murmured. His mother's desertion had created a void in his life that he still hadn't managed to fill. He reached into his back pocket and withdrew his wallet, then pulled out the photo he'd found as a child. For years he'd thought of his mother as his own personal angel watching over him from heaven. And then, one day, that had all changed. He'd gone down to the local pub to drag his father home. There, he'd found him drunk and blathering to the other patrons about his "dead" wife.

Seamus hadn't known Sean was there and had regaled the patrons seated around him with a story of how he'd found his wife with another man, then kicked her out of his house. The car accident that had killed her a few years later had been divine punishment for her adultery.

Sean remembered running out of the pub, running and running until his lungs burned and he'd gasped for breath. He'd been betrayed and deceived by his angel, as if all the love he'd given her had been a lie. And he'd carried that feeling around with him since then—even after his mother had returned.

Fiona Quinn had come back into their lives nearly two years ago, along with Keely, the sister they'd never known. His brothers had welcomed their return, even forgiven their father for telling the story of Fiona's demise. But Sean couldn't forgive so easily—or trust the love that Fiona seemed so determined to shower on her family.

If he couldn't love his own mother, how was he supposed to love anyone else? The answers didn't come easily—and the questions never seemed to stop.

3

BY THE TIME Laurel pulled up in front of the Rand mansion, it was nearly five in the evening. She hid a yawn behind her hand and tried to stretch the kinks out of her neck. The flight from Honolulu to Los Angeles and then to Boston had been a grind and she was ready for a hot shower and soft bed.

Her solitary honeymoon had been exactly what she'd needed to come to grips with what had happened on her wedding day. Laurel turned off the ignition and rested her hands on the steering wheel. Edward's deception had been bad enough, but considering her reaction to Sean Quinn, maybe it was best that her fiancé had skipped the wedding.

She'd thought a marriage without love would be at least tolerable. Edward was charming and intelligent and he'd seemed to genuinely care about her. But just one evening spent with Sean Quinn had been enough to show her how wrong she'd been.

Passions she hadn't known she possessed had suddenly surfaced. Every time Sean had touched her, her heart had beat a little faster and her knees had turned to jelly. Edward had never caused such a reaction. One kiss from her stand-in bridegroom had proved that fact.

Gathering the last ounce of her energy, Laurel

stepped out of her car. Her bags seemed to weigh a ton as she dragged them to the front door. She punched the code into the security system, then opened the door, pulling her bags in behind her.

As she glanced around the foyer, her thoughts returned to her wedding night. A tiny shiver raced through her as she remembered that last kiss; Sean trapping her against the wall, overwhelming her with his lips and his hands. A groan slipped from her throat.

"Welcome home, Miss Laurel."

Laurel jumped at the sound of Alistair's chipper voice, a tiny scream slipping from her throat. She turned as he hurried toward her. Hefting up her bags, he smiled warmly. "And where is Mr. Edward?"

"What are you doing here?" Laurel asked.

"Your uncle decided to stay here for a time. He heard about a coin auction at Sotheby's in New York City and was anxious to attend, so he decided not to go back to Maine until later this month. You look very tired. Isn't Mr. Edward with you?"

She scrambled to make up an excuse for her absent husband. Her uncle's presence had not been part of the plan! "I—I dropped him off at his apartment so he could pack up a few of his things. He didn't have time before the wedding. I'm going to go back into town to pick him up in an hour."

"And how was your honeymoon? Very romantic, I trust."

"Oh, very! We had a...a wonderful time," she said, trying to sound enthusiastic. "The beaches were beautiful and I—we walked every day." Laurel had never been an accomplished liar and Alistair was a shrewd man. A quick retreat was in order before he suspected the truth. "I—I better go pick up Edward."

"I thought you said he'd be expecting you in an hour."

She forced a smile. "Well, the honeymoon isn't over. I can't stand being away from him for a single second." Laurel backed toward the door, then slipped out and hurried to her car. "Damn," she muttered. "Damn, damn, damn." Now what was she supposed to do? She'd never anticipated this wrinkle in her plan.

Over the past two weeks in Hawaii, she'd formulated a perfect strategy. She'd collect her inheritance, wait a few months, then write to her uncle to tell him that the marriage had been a mistake. She'd even decided to use the real Edward's past to her advantage. She'd married a con man who was already married. So, she'd fulfilled the requirements to get her trust fund— technically. The only part that worried her was that her uncle could be a capricious man and he might decide that a failed marriage wasn't a marriage at all.

"I need a husband," she muttered to herself as she pulled out of the driveway. "I have a husband. A bought-and-paid-for husband. I just have to find him."

As she drove toward Boston, Laurel rummaged through her purse for her cell phone. The information operator answered and Laurel requested the phone number for Sean Quinn. "I'm sorry, ma'am, I don't have a listing for Sean Quinn."

"Try S. Quinn."

"No, ma'am."

Laurel groaned. How could she have been so stupid? For ten thousand dollars, she should have at least requested his phone number. There had to be some way to find the man. "What about Quinn's Pub?" she asked. "It's in South Boston."

She waited for a few moments, holding her breath until the operator came on the line. "Here's the number." An automated voice recited the digits and Laurel quickly committed them to memory before she dialed. A minute later she had the address of the pub and directions on how to get there.

Until now, seeing Sean again had never been an option. But after what had happened between them, Laurel had fantasized about another encounter—nearly every waking moment of her "honeymoon." She'd nearly asked him to come with her to Hawaii that night, as they'd said their farewells, and regretted not doing so.

As she wove through traffic, she tried to formulate the best approach to her problem. Ten thousand dollars had been a high price to pay for one day's work. Maybe she could convince him that he owed her more time. If he requested more money, she might be able to find a few hundred. The money she'd given him had been the last from her wedding fund, a reasonable expense she'd thought. Or maybe she could convince him to wait for a cut of her trust fund.

When she pulled up in front of the pub, Laurel said a quick prayer, hoping that she'd find him quickly. She glanced at her reflection in the rearview mirror, then grabbed her purse and dashed on a bit of lipstick. Satisfied that she looked as good as a jet-lagged honeymooner could look, she stepped out of the car and hurried inside.

Lively Irish music played. A beautiful wood bar, reminiscent of nineteenth-century pubs, ran along one wall, its mirror reflecting the dim lighting. On her only visit to Dublin on a college summer vacation, she'd visited pubs just like Quinn's. A white-haired barkeep nodded at her as she approached.

"I'm hoping you might know where I can find Sean Quinn."

"And what would you be wantin' with Sean?" the man asked, his Irish accent thick.

"I have a private matter I need to discuss," Laurel said. "Do you know how I can reach him?"

"I wouldn't know that. Why don't you leave him a note and if he comes in I'll—"

"No," Laurel said, growing impatient with the runaround. "I have to find him now."

The man shook his head. "I don't know who you think you are, but—"

"I'm his wife," Laurel blurted. The old man froze, his expression a mask of astonishment, and she silently cursed her quick tongue. She hadn't meant to say it, but she needed to find Sean. "Not exactly his wife, but—"

"One minute," the man interrupted. "I'll just ring him." He hurried off to the far end of the bar and, after a short phone conversation, returned to her. "He's on his way."

"Thank you," Laurel said, a knot tightening in her stomach. Her hands flitted to her hair and she nervously smoothed the wrinkled skirt of her sundress. If she was going to make this work, she needed to control her rash behavior. All her life, she'd been too impulsive, too reckless, never looking before she leaped. That's what had gotten her into this mess in the first place—marrying a man she didn't even know.

She glanced up and found the bartender watching her with a suspicious glint in his eye. "Can I get you anything to drink, lass?"

"White wine would be nice," she said.

As she sipped her drink, Laurel casually observed her surroundings. In the rear of the pub, stained-glass lamps illuminated a pool table and dartboards hung from the walls. A chalkboard menu near the bar boasted Irish favorites including corned beef and cabbage, Irish stew and something called Dublin Coddle.

Laurel's stomach growled and she realized that she hadn't eaten for nearly six hours. She waved to the bartender and he approached, this time a bit more warily. "I'd like to order something to eat. Some soup?"

"We've got a nice potato soup. Or maybe ye'd prefer pea and ham soup. We also might have some clam chowder left from yesterday."

"Potato, please," Laurel said.

"Let me get you a bowl."

After he left, Laurel gulped down the rest of her wine, hoping that it might fortify her courage. She'd paid Sean to pose as her bridegroom for a day and he had no obligation to help her. How could she convince him to resume his role? What kind of offer might he accept?

Laurel wasn't certain how much a woman ought to pay for a husband but figured it couldn't be more than the man would make at a day-to-day job. After all, the job wasn't that difficult. She'd start with twenty thousand and negotiate from there. Twenty thousand out of five million was a small price to pay.

"Here you go, lass. Potato soup. And that's soda bread." He rested his arms on the bar and watched her eat. "Tell me, when did you and my son get married?"

The spoonful of potato soup was halfway down her throat when the old man posed the question. Laurel coughed, snatching up her napkin. Her eyes began to water and Sean's father reached across the bar and slapped her on the back. "Your...your son?"

"Sean is my son. I'm Seamus Quinn. And you'd be?"

"Laurel Rand."

"I'm surprised that Sean didn't tell us he'd found himself a wife. But then, the boy never did talk much."

"Well, I'm not exactly his wife. Not technically." She quickly stood and grabbed her purse, wiping at her runny eyes. "Will you excuse me? I'll be right back."

The ladies' room was in the rear of the bar, past the pool table. When she got inside, she locked the door behind her, then stood in front of the mirror and wiped at the smudged mascara beneath her eyes. "Calm down," she murmured. "If he accepts your offer, then you'll be fine. And if he refuses, you'll deal with it."

With a soft curse, she opened her purse and pulled out her cosmetics bag. A tiny vial contained her favorite perfume and she dabbed a bit on before pulling out her mascara and lipstick. She'd have to use every advantage that she had, including scented skin, smouldering eyes and a sexy mouth.

SEAN STEPPED INSIDE Quinn's Pub and scanned the bar for his father. Seamus had called ten minutes before, frantic, insisting that Sean come down to the pub immediately. He'd claimed an emergency but had refused to give details, so Sean had no choice but to leave the Red Sox game he'd been watching on television and head down to the bar a few hours early.

When he walked in, he'd assumed that the crowd had been too much for Seamus to handle and he'd needed an extra pair of hands. But the Saturday evening crowd was about what he'd expected for the early hour. Sean ducked beneath the end of the bar. As he nabbed an apron and wrapped it around his waist, he saw his father hurrying toward him from the back of the pub.

"Good, you're here," he muttered.

"What's wrong?"

Seamus grabbed him by the elbow and pulled him closer. "She's here. In the toilet."

"Who is here?"

"Yer wife. She and I had a little chin-wag and the lass says yer married."

Sean frowned. Lately, women had gone to greater lengths to entice the last remaining Quinn brother, but this was— Oh, hell. Could his father be talking about Laurel Rand? "What did she look like, Da?"

"Like a woman who just caught herself a husband."

"Blonde? Wavy hair?" He held his hand up to his chin. "About so tall?"

"Said her name was Laurie or—"

Sean didn't bother with the rest of the conversation with his father. He yanked off the apron, tossed it on the bar and headed for the ladies' room. When he'd left Laurel that night after the wedding, he'd told himself it was the last he'd see of her. And though he was curious about the attraction he'd felt for her, he knew better than to dwell on it. He wasn't ready to fall in love and he suspected he never would be.

The door to the ladies' room swung open an instant before he reached for the knob. Laurel stood in front of him, wide-eyed and wary. Sean searched for something to say. A variety of opening lines raced through his head and he opened his mouth, ready to give one of them a try. What was it about Laurel? One minute, conversation with her was so easy, the next, he lost all capacity to speak, all ability to think straight.

Suddenly, Laurel threw her arms around his neck and kissed him. At first he was too stunned to reciprocate. But when her lips parted slightly, Sean didn't see any reason not to enjoy what she offered. He slipped his hands around her waist and pulled her nearer, deepening the kiss until she went soft in his arms. And when Laurel finally pulled away, her face was flushed and her eyes bright. A tiny smile twitched at the corners of her mouth, so she was obviously satisfied with his response.

"Hello," Sean said.

"Hi. I suppose you're wondering what I'm doing here."

"No." In truth, from the instant his mouth met hers, he hadn't cared why she'd come. The kiss was a good enough reason. Over the past two weeks he'd nearly forgotten what she tasted like, how she felt in his arms. And it hadn't taken much to bring it back. One kiss.

"No?"

"Well, maybe," Sean said. "How was Hawaii?"

"Sunny, warm, beautiful. As the only single woman renting a honeymoon bungalow, I felt a little out of place. But I needed the time away. And it was a nice way to celebrate my twenty-sixth birthday."

Sean reached out and tucked an errant strand of her hair behind her ear. "Happy birthday."

"Thanks," she said. "Another year older, but not any wiser."

"Laurel, what are you doing here?"

"I—I just wanted to see you." She paused, then shook her head. "That's not true. Uncle Sinclair has moved into the mansion for a while. Something about a coin auction in New York. Of course, he'd never think to rent a hotel room when I've got eight empty bedrooms."

"Have you told him about Edward?"

She shifted uneasily. "I need a favor. I know I said you'd just have to pose as my groom for a day, but I think I might need you for a little longer. And I was wondering if I could...rent you for a few more weeks?"

"Rent me?"

"Hire you. I just need you to be my husband again." She grabbed his hand and pulled him into the ladies' room. "There's something I didn't tell you the day of the wedding," Laurel admitted. "I wasn't just worried about the embarrassment. I needed to get married that day."

Sean's gaze automatically dropped to her belly. "You're pregnant?"

"No!" Laurel cried. "I had to get married before my twenty-sixth birthday so I could get the five million dollars from my trust fund," she blurted. "My uncle is the administrator of the trust that my father left me when he died. He seems to think I can't handle the money unless I'm married."

"So this wasn't about humiliation?" Sean asked. "It was about money." The woman he thought he'd "married" disappeared in front of his eyes. He now knew the attraction they'd shared had been nothing more than an act fueled by a mercenary nature.

"I need that money. Now. If I don't marry, then I have to wait until I'm thirty-one. That's five years from now and I can't wait."

"Not enough money for designer fashions and expensive jewelry?" Sean asked, a sarcastic edge to his voice.

"No! That's not it."

He'd been so captivated by her honesty and now he found that had all been a facade. She wasn't any different than any other woman—only interested in what he could do for her, what he might give her, what she could take. Sean shoved his hands into the back pockets of his jeans to keep himself from touching her again. He shouldn't have trusted her. He knew better than to trust a woman—even one as beautiful as Laurel Rand. "What are you offering?"

She seemed taken aback by his question, but Sean didn't regret asking. If this was all about money, then he'd be damned if he was going to offer his services for free.

"I've thought about that. We'd have to negotiate reasonable compensation. And we can do that later. For now, I need you to get your things and come home with me."

Sean leaned back against the bathroom door and observed her shrewdly. He'd wondered over the past few weeks whether he'd fallen victim to the Quinn family curse, whether coming to Laurel's rescue that day might cost him his freedom. But he was happy to see that he'd battled the curse and come up the winner. There was no way this scheming woman would ever capture his heart.

"Not until we come to terms," he said. "How long will my services be required?"

"At least a month," she said.

"My day rate is five hundred dollars," he said, padding the figure a bit. "Thirty days at five hundred is fifteen thousand. Of course, expenses are extra."

"Your day rate? Are you a plumber?"

"I'm a private investigator," Sean said. "Remember?"

"Right! That's perfect then. Five hundred a day, plus expenses, limited to an additional five thousand." She held out her hand and he shook it.

Her fingers were warm and delicate in his hand and, for a moment, Sean didn't want to let go. Cursing inwardly, he pulled his hand away. "It's a deal."

"Good, then let's go. We'll have to get your things. I told Alistair we'd be back in an hour. That gives us just enough time to get our story straight."

Sean nodded, then opened the bathroom door, stepping aside to let her pass. As they walked through the pub, he let his hand rest on the small of her back. It was something a husband would do. He'd seen his brothers do the same for the women they loved. Yet when he touched Laurel, it was easy to forget that everything between them was a charade.

"I'm leaving, Da," Sean shouted. "I won't be back for a few weeks. Give Rudy a call. He'll fill in for me."

"Yah can't leave me in the lurch!" Seamus shouted.

"You'll be fine," he murmured.

Laurel's car was parked in front of the bar. She circled around to the driver's side and Sean followed her, then held out his hand. "What?" she asked.

"Keys. I'm the husband. The husband always drives."

"Not in this marriage. My car is very temperamental."

"Are we going to have our first argument?"

Grudgingly, she slapped the keys into his hand and walked around to the passenger side. Sean slipped behind the wheel, then reached over to unlock her door. But she didn't open it. "Get in," he said.

She peered through the window, rapping on it with her knuckles. "Husbands open car doors for their wives."

Sean groaned. For a guy who wasn't really married, he was already following orders like a henpecked spouse. He crawled back out of the car, jogged around to Laurel's side and yanked open the door. "Make sure you complain about my driving," he suggested. "And give me all the wrong directions. Isn't that what wives do?"

As he shut her door, Sean suppressed a grin. Maybe this "marriage" would be just what he needed—to convince himself that marriage would never be an option for the only remaining Quinn bachelor.

THEY RETURNED to the house an hour later, Alistair welcoming them both at the front door. He reached to take Sean's duffel, but Sean shook his head and insisted on carrying it upstairs. Laurel made a mental note to tell her "husband" that he'd need to be especially careful around Alistair. The butler was fiercely loyal to Sinclair and any suspicions on his part would be immediately relayed to her uncle.

"I've taken the liberty of preparing a light meal for you," Alistair said, following them both up the stairs. "Sandwiches, a roasted vegetable salad and a fresh blueberry crumble. I've put it in your bedroom. Mr. Sinclair would like you to join him for brandy in the library after you've settled in."

He opened the door to Laurel's bedroom and walked inside, switching on a lamp next to the small sofa. "Would you like me to unpack for you?" Alistair asked Sean.

"No, I can take care of that." Sean reached for his wallet, but Laurel grabbed his arm to stop him.

"We'll be fine," she said. "Let Uncle know that we'll be down in twenty minutes. Thank you, Alistair."

When the butler had left the room, she heard Sean release a tightly held breath. "I was going to tip him," he said. "That wasn't right?"

"No, Alistair is an employee of my uncle Sinclair. But he takes care of me—and you now—because he wants to. Not because he has to."

She crossed the room to the small sofa set in an alcove. Alistair had set out the tray on a tea table beside it. She picked up one of Alistair's famous cucumber-

and-cream-cheese sandwiches and took a bite. "Are you hungry? Alistair is a really good cook."

"No," he said. He stood in the center of the room as if he wasn't sure what he should do.

Laurel moved to the dresser, pulled open the top drawer, then scooped out all her underwear. "You can use this for your clothes. I'll clean out another drawer if you need it. And there's plenty of room in the closet." She looked down at her underwear, then walked over to the wardrobe, pulled open the door and tossed the lingerie inside. "The bathroom is through there." Laurel pointed to the door. "You'll need to change before we go downstairs."

Sean looked down at the clothes he was wearing. "What's wrong with what I have on?"

Laurel let her gaze drift down from his handsome face to his long, lean body. He wore a T-shirt and jeans like no other man could; the T-shirt stretched tight over his muscled chest, the black jeans riding low on his hips. "Uncle insists that everyone dress for the evening."

"We're having a drink."

"It's after six. It's one of his rules. Now, what did you bring along?"

"Jeans, T-shirts." Sean strode over to the bed and rummaged through his duffel. He pulled out a black sweater and held it up. "How about this?"

"You don't have a jacket and tie?"

"I don't own a jacket and tie," Sean said. "Whenever I need to dress up, I borrow something from my brother Brian."

"We'll have to shop tomorrow." She crossed to the closet. "I think Edward may have left something here."

"I'm not wearing his clothes." He grabbed his duffel and crossed the room to the dresser. But before he put his clothes inside, he held out a stray piece of her lingerie. A lacy red bra.

A blush warming her cheeks, Laurel grabbed it from his hand. She took his sweater, as well, and smoothed her hand over the fine silk knit. The designer label was a surprise.

"My sister-in-law gave it to me for Christmas. I've never worn it."

"This will be fine. We'll buy you some new things when we get a chance."

He grabbed the hem of his T-shirt and yanked it over his head. It happened so quickly that Laurel didn't have a chance to prepare, or to find something else to occupy her eyes. Her gaze fell to his chest, smooth and finely muscled. He was lean and hard, yet Laurel suspected it didn't come from working out at a health club. He just didn't seem the type.

She swallowed hard, then handed him the sweater. "We...we need to get our story straight about the honeymoon. I think you should let me do most of the talking. Add a few details here and there, but don't say too much."

"I never do," Sean replied.

"And we need to discuss public displays of affection. We have to appear...comfortable with each other. Uncle Sinclair needs to see that we're in love, but we shouldn't hang all over each other. Uncle has very old-fashioned ideas about decorum and propriety."

"Tell me what to do," Sean said.

"Well, we can hold hands," she suggested.

He reached out and took her hand, then wove his fingers through hers. His touch sent a current through her body, so strong that she had to fight the impulse to pull away.

"How's that?" he asked.

"Good. And you can touch me in other ways. Put your arm around me."

He slipped his other arm around her waist. "Like this?" he asked as he pulled her close, her hand pinned behind her back.

"And...and then, you could..."

"Kiss you?" he asked, pressing his lips to her cheek.

"Yes."

He moved to her neck and a wave of sensation washed through her as he bit softly. "How about here?"

A ragged breath slipped from her throat. "I think that would be a little...too...oh, that feels good."

He suddenly pulled away, as if the contact hadn't fazed him at all. "Maybe that's going too far."

Laurel blinked, then nodded. "You're right. Touching is fine. A kiss on the cheek occasionally. But nothing else." She stepped away from him and sat on the sofa, pressing her hands between her knees to keep them from trembling. "If Uncle asks you strange questions, just go along. Answer as best you can. He never stays on one subject for too long."

"He shouldn't be hard to trick. When do you think he'll give you your money?"

"I don't want to trick him. The money is mine. My

father left it to me. He just made the mistake of naming Uncle Sinclair as administrator of the trust, so Sinclair makes up the rules about when I can have the money. I need it now."

"Why do you need it now?"

"I just do," Laurel said. She'd never told anyone about her plans for the arts center. Until now, it had been a dream. She'd filled notebooks with her ideas, everything from curriculum to design of the classrooms to the teachers she'd try to hire. But she was almost superstitious about telling anyone, worried that any negative comment might ruin her perfect dream. "My reasons are my own," she said. "And they're none of your business."

Sean shrugged. "Just curious." He slipped the sweater over his head, then raked his hands through his hair. "I think we're ready."

Laurel strode to the door. "All right, Edward. Uncle Sinclair gets impatient when he's kept waiting."

As she walked down the wide staircase, Laurel tried to calm her frustration. She'd thought it would be easy to carry out the charade. Once Sinclair was certain she and "Edward" had married for the right reasons, he'd turn over her money. He wouldn't dare make her give it back once the marriage failed.

She didn't like to lie, but the deception was necessary and it was for a good cause. She could have waited for another man to come along. But who knows when that might have happened? And how was she supposed to trust her own judgment, especially after the mistake she'd made with Edward? She certainly didn't want to wait another five years for the money.

When she reached the bottom of the stairs, Laurel waited. Sean joined her a few seconds later. He reached out and took her hand, slipping his fingers between hers. "Lead on," he said.

They found Sinclair sitting in the huge leather wing chair in the library. Alistair had set out the brandy on a small side table and now stood silently in the shadows. As they entered, Laurel's uncle didn't bother to acknowledge them. Instead he kept his nose buried in a book.

Laurel sat on the leather sofa and motioned Sean to sit beside her. Alistair fetched them both a brandy, then resumed his place. After five minutes Sinclair finally glanced up, as if surprised that she and Sean were in the room. "Here you are then," he said, staring at Laurel. "I hope you used sunscreen."

"The weather was beautiful in Hawaii, Uncle."

"Beautiful," Sean repeated.

"Did you see any birds?"

"There were lots of birds there," Laurel said. "You would have found some new species to put on your list, Uncle. Uncle is only interested in American birds, Edward. But Hawaii is a state, so all those birds count."

He turned to Sean. "Do you like birds, Edward?"

"I do. I like ducks. Sparrows. And cardinals."

"A cardinal was the first bird I put on my list," he said. He looked down at his book again and for a long time didn't look up. Laurel took a sip of her brandy, then glanced over at Sean and shrugged.

"You like coins?" Sean asked.

Sinclair didn't answer, acting as if he hadn't heard. But Laurel knew better. He was testing Sean—*Edward*.

"What's your favorite coin?"

Sinclair slapped the book shut and, for a moment, Laurel thought he was angry, perturbed that Sean had interrupted his reading. "Let me show you," he said. "Alistair, bring out the Seated Liberty."

Laurel gave Sean's hand a squeeze. Her uncle loved to discuss his coin collection with anyone who would listen. And now, he had a fresh set of ears. She slowly stood and walked over to the tall cases of books, searching through the titles as she listened to Sinclair talk about the history behind the coin.

"This is a very rare coin," he said. "It was minted in 1866. There's only one other in better condition and it goes up for auction next week."

Sean seemed genuinely interested and when Sinclair brought out another coin, he pulled up a footstool and sat next to Sinclair so he could examine the coin more closely. Laurel watched him in the low light of the library, taken by how sweet he could be. How had a man like Sean Quinn managed to remain single for so long?

"This is my Liberty Capped cent," Sinclair said. "Look at those luster darts. This coin was made in 1794 and the machinery was primitive at best, so perfection is nearly impossible. This is only one of three which is graded mint."

"Wow," Sean said. "It looks brand new."

"Laurel!" Sinclair called. "Get the Breen. The copy I gave you for Christmas in 1991."

Laurel retrieved the book from the shelf where she kept it and handed it to her uncle.

"If you're interested in coins, then this is the book." Sinclair patted the cover. *"The Complete Encyclopedia of U.S. and Colonial Coins."*

"So, you only collect U.S. coins?"

"And Colonials," Sinclair said. "And U.S. stamps. A collector has to have some limits. That way, you don't waste money chasing things you don't really need or want." He held the coins out to Alistair, then pushed to his feet. "We'll talk again, Edward. You're an interesting young man."

"Thank you, sir," Sean said, quickly standing.

Laurel watched her uncle walk out of the room, Alistair trailing behind him, then smiled. "He gave you Breen."

"Is that good?" Sean asked.

"It's just a big book of coins, but it's like his bible. He spends hours pouring over that book. I think he must have it memorized by now."

Sean nodded, then tucked the book under his arm. "He's not going to give me a test, is he?"

Laurel giggled. "He might. But not right away." She paused, then pushed up on her toes and gave him a quick kiss on her cheek. "You're a good husband."

A tiny smile quirked his lips and he shrugged. "That's what I get paid for."

Laurel's breath caught in her throat. For a moment she'd forgotten that this was all just an act, that the handsome man standing next to her wasn't really her husband at all. "I guess it's time for bed," she murmured.

Sean held up the book. "I know what I'll do if I can't sleep." He slipped his arm around her waist as they walked out of the library and up the stairs. Laurel knew there was no need for the oddly possessive gesture. No one was watching. But she liked the way it felt when he touched her, the illusion of affection that it gave her.

But what would happen once the door to her bedroom closed? Would they continue this charade of romance or would it be strictly business? With each step, her heart beat a little faster in anticipation. This was the wedding night she hadn't had. And Laurel was afraid that morning would come all too fast.

4

SEAN SLOWLY CLOSED the door of Laurel's bedroom and leaned back against it, watching as she walked over to the huge four-poster bed. Her room, like the rest of the mansion, was richly furnished with expensive antiques and beautiful fabrics, a far cry from the tattered furnishings of the house on Kilgore Street or the hodgepodge decor of his flat in Southie.

Again and again, he'd been reminded of the two very different worlds they'd come from. The ten-thousand-dollar check in his wallet represented a fortune to him, a chance to build his business. Yet, to Laurel, it was spare change, payment for a day's work, and there was more where that came from. He couldn't really blame her. Given a chance at five million, Sean probably would have risked more than just money.

As she wandered around the room, his gaze followed her, taking in her slender body and beautiful features. He'd known a lot of women who were pretty, but Laurel's beauty eclipsed them all. She wasn't like the women he usually met. She was…classy. Smart. Sophisticated. And way out of his league.

"I think tonight went well," she murmured, running a finger over a little china rabbit that sat on her bedside table.

"Do you think he suspects?" Sean asked, setting the book he carried on the table near the sofa.

She quickly turned, concern etching her features. "Do you?"

Sean shrugged. Their audience with Uncle Sinclair had been strange at best. The old man didn't appear to be interested in the state of his niece's marriage. He'd barely noticed that Laurel was in the room, so occupied was he with his coins. But Sean knew better. "Your uncle wants you to believe he's not the full shilling."

"Full shilling?" Laurel asked. "Is that a coin joke?"

"It's my da's expression. Sinclair doesn't have all his oars in the water. He's a few sandwiches short of a picnic. He's—"

"I get it," Laurel said. "Maybe he is a little...crazy."

"But he's not crazy. He just wants you to believe he is. I think he's a pretty shrewd old guy."

Laurel fussed with the bedcovers, pulling them back and then smoothing them out until they were perfectly turned down. "I've never been able to figure him out. My mother died when I was ten and my father when I was nineteen, and Uncle Sinclair's been in charge of everything since then. He's the only family I have." Her shoulders rose and dropped. "I'm not even sure how he feels about me."

"Does it make a difference?" Sean asked.

She sat on the edge of the bed and rested her hands in her lap, studying her fingernails. Sean fought the urge to cross the room to sit beside her, to take her hands in his. All evening, he'd played the proper husband, touching her every now and then, smiling when she spoke, holding her hand as they talked with her uncle. It had seemed so natural, but now that they were alone, he couldn't bring himself to do the same. Where did the act end and the real desire begin?

"It would be nice to know there's someone in the world who really cares about me," she continued. "You have your family. They must love you very much. That has to make you feel good."

Sean's thoughts turned to his mother. Though he knew he could always count on his father and five brothers, he still hadn't resolved his issues with Fiona Quinn. "I guess so," he murmured.

It would be so easy to trust Laurel, to open up to her and to talk about problems he'd always kept to himself. But Sean had to remember Laurel was a woman and, like Fiona, she couldn't be fully trusted.

"Tell me about your family," Laurel asked.

Sean pushed away from the door and crossed the room. He grabbed up his duffel bag and finished unpacking, laying T-shirts and boxer shorts on a nearby chair. "We don't need to talk," he said.

A long silence fell over the room, Laurel's expression grim. His words caused him a pang of regret and Sean dropped what he was doing and sat next to her. Hesitantly, he reached out and took her fingers, twisting them through his as he spoke. "I'm sorry. I'm just not much for that kind of conversation. Sports, the weather, current events. I can handle that."

"No, you're right. There's no reason for us to discuss personal matters. I have to remember, you're just doing a job."

"That's what you wanted, isn't it?"

Laurel nodded, then snatched her fingers from his

and rose. "I'm going to take a shower—or maybe you'd like to use the bathroom first?"

"No, go ahead," Sean said. He glanced around the room. "What are the sleeping arrangements here?"

Laurel's gaze darted to the four-poster. For a moment he thought she might invite him to share the bed with her. Though the prospect was intriguing, he knew better than to tempt fate. He quickly pointed to a small reading alcove near the other side of the room. "I can take the sofa over there."

"No, you can have the bed," she said, grabbing a folded throw from a nearby chair. "That sofa is too small for—"

He took the throw from her hands, then picked up a pillow, as well. "I sleep on my sofa at home all the time. It won't be a problem. If it's uncomfortable, I can always stretch out on the floor."

She grabbed the robe lying across the end of the bed and clutched it to her chest. "All right then, I'm just going to take my shower."

The door to the bathroom closed and Sean let out a tightly held breath. He'd thought this job would be easy, but the tension that had sprung up between them made every minute alone together sheer torture. He almost wanted to return to the library and an audience with Uncle Sinclair.

Sean moved to the door of the bathroom and listened to the sound of running water. A vision of Laurel flashed in his head and he let it linger, imagining her as she undressed and stepped into the shower...as she let the water sluice over her naked body...smoothed her soap-slicked hands over her—

Sean cursed then strode away from the door. This was crazy! Nothing, not even twenty thousand dollars, was worth this kind of punishment. How could she expect him to live with her as her husband and not think about the pleasures that a husband usually shared with his wife?

He ran his fingers through his hair, then turned for the door. He wasn't about to hang around until she came out of the bathroom, her skin still damp from her shower, her robe clinging to her body. He'd find something else to occupy his time until she crawled into bed and turned off the lights.

The hallway was silent as he walked down the sweeping staircase. His footsteps made little noise against the thick Oriental runner. When he reached the door to the kitchen, he shoved it open, then stopped, surprised to see Alistair still up.

The diminutive man looked over his shoulder and smiled at Sean as he walked toward the sink. "I thought you'd gone to bed," he said.

"Strange house," Sean said. "I'm not going to sleep. It will take me a few nights to settle in."

"Perhaps I can prepare something for you. A snack?"

"Do you have any beer?"

Alistair nodded and retrieved two bottles from the huge commercial refrigerator. He popped the caps off with an opener. "Would you like a glass?"

Sean grabbed one of the bottles and took a long swallow, then shook his head. "Nope. I'm fine." He held up the bottle. "Guinness."

Alistair carefully poured his beer into a half-pint

glass. "I enjoy a bit of the black stuff every now and then."

"My da has an Irish pub in Southie and—" Sean swallowed the rest of his sentence, realizing too late that he'd blown his cover. "I mean, I've been to a pub in—"

"No need," Alistair said. "I'm aware of your charade."

Sean cursed inwardly, but tried to maintain a calm facade. "Charade? I don't know what you mean."

"You might tell me your name," Alistair said.

"It's Edward. Edward Garland Wilson." The butler raised an eyebrow and Sean knew he was made. "It *is*." The butler shook his head. "All right. It's Sean Quinn. How did you know?"

"You were nothing like Laurel described. I knew how much pressure her uncle put on her to marry and how desperate she was to get her trust fund. What happened to Edward?"

"He didn't make it to the wedding," he said.

"I wasn't sure that he existed at all. And how did you come to be mixed up in this little drama of Miss Laurel's?"

"She needed a husband. She made me an offer I couldn't refuse."

Alistair nodded. "Ah. *The Godfather.* One of my favorite American films. I suppose you could say that Miss Laurel has decided to go to the mattresses?" He chuckled softly. "I'm not surprised. That is precisely like Miss Laurel."

"I guess she's used to getting her way," Sean murmured.

"Oh, no," Alistair said. "Miss Laurel is quite unspoiled. But she does have a tendency to set her sights on something and then rush headlong into it without thinking about the consequences first. She's headstrong, yes, and single-minded. But not at all selfish." He glanced at Sean over the rim of his glass, then licked the foam off his upper lip. "I can't say that I blame Miss Laurel. Sinclair Rand toys with her as a cat toys with a mouse. She didn't have an easy childhood and Sinclair hasn't made her adulthood much better. It's been a battle of wills between them for years."

"How so?" Sean asked, his curiosity piqued.

"Laurel's mother died when she was ten and her father nine years later. It was very difficult for her, even more so when Sinclair became the authority figure in her life."

"I lost my mother when I was three," Sean said. "That can mess a kid up for a long time."

"Then you understand."

They drank their beer silently, the two of them lost in their thoughts for a few minutes. Alistair seemed to know Laurel better than anyone, even her uncle, and Sean was grateful for any insight into his "wife." "What happened to Laurel's parents?"

"Laurel's father, Stewart Rand, was wealthy and older when he married Miss Louise. She was a dancer and an actress. He and his brother, Sinclair, had made the family fortune and Mr. Stewart was determined to enjoy it in his later years. Sinclair didn't approve of Louise Carpenter. There was twenty-five years difference in age between them and he considered her an unsuitable choice, from a working-class family."

"And she died?"

"Miss Louise died of cancer three days after their twelfth wedding anniversary. Laurel and her mother were so close, they did everything together. Her mother had her in ballet lessons and theater class. They studied painting and sculpting. When most little girls were playing with dolls, Miss Louise took Laurel to museums and operas and symphony concerts. I once thought Laurel was destined for a career on the stage. But after Miss Louise died, that all stopped. Mr. Stewart lost all interest in the child and she was left to fend for herself. Mr. Stewart passed on nine years later. He had a heart attack shortly after Laurel left for college. Perhaps he thought he'd finished raising Laurel and he could finally join his wife."

"And then Sinclair was in charge," Sean commented.

"He looked upon her as if she were a nuisance, an embarrassment, a reminder that his brother had succumbed to his baser instincts. Once Laurel was out of the house, she began to blossom, she began dancing again and painting, she appeared in several plays. But Sinclair insisted that she get a proper degree in something practical. He decided she needed a teaching degree, and if she refused to take the classes, then he'd refuse to pay for her education. Every time she took a step away from him, he'd drag her back."

"I didn't know Laurel was a teacher."

Alistair nodded. "Up until last June, she taught music at a grade school in Dorchester. She loves teaching, loves the children. I thought she'd finally found her place in the world, but then she decided to marry and quit her job. That was quite a surprise."

It took a moment for Sean to absorb the news. He'd just assumed that Laurel lived off her family's money, that she was nothing more than a spoiled rich girl determined to have her way. "Why is it so important for her to get her inheritance?"

Alistair shrugged. "Perhaps the money represents independence for her. She could move out of the house and start a life of her own, make a break from Sinclair. But as much as she wants to break away, he wants to hold on to her. I think, in his own way, he's grown fond of her."

Sean straightened. "Are you going to tell Sinclair about us?"

The butler shook his head. "This is between Miss Laurel and her uncle. You've just managed to get caught in the middle. We'll just have to see how events unfold, won't we?"

Grabbing up his beer, Sean nodded. "We will." He paused, then smiled at Alistair. "It was nice talking to you."

"Good night, Mr. Edward."

As Sean wandered through the dark house, he was forced to admit that his assumptions about Laurel and her motives might have been wrong. That this wasn't about greed at all. He'd been pretty quick to jump to conclusions. For now, he'd give her the benefit of the doubt. After all, she was his "wife." It was the least he could do.

LAUREL ROLLED OVER and punched her pillow, unable to get comfortable. Though she should have been completely exhausted, she felt as if every nerve in her body was on edge. She'd expected Sean to be lying on the sofa when she emerged from the bathroom, but he'd been gone. Frantic, she'd hurried down the stairs only to hear his voice coming from the kitchen.

"Relax," she murmured. "He's not going to run away."

But then, maybe twenty thousand hadn't been enough. She could offer him more, since she really didn't have the twenty thousand anyway. Her only chance to pay him was if her plan succeeded and Sinclair turned over her trust fund. And if that happened, then a few thousand more wouldn't matter one way or the other.

With a groan, she pulled the pillow over her face. A month of nights with Sean Quinn sleeping in her room. A month of days watching him move, listening to his voice, staring into his handsome face. A woman only had so much self-control! Though she hadn't been in love with Edward, she'd liked him enough to marry him. Laurel had convinced herself to be pragmatic about passion.

Since there hadn't been much heat between her and Edward, she hadn't had to worry. In truth, she'd considered their lack of a sex life to be proof that they had a friendship first. And Edward had insisted that they save themselves for marriage, a request she thought chivalrous. Laurel frowned. "That should have made me suspicious," she muttered. "No man in his right mind passes up sex when he has a willing and available woman."

But then, maybe it wasn't Edward. Maybe it was her. Maybe she'd unconsciously been unwilling to release her passionate side. She'd seen how her mother's death had nearly destroyed her father. For nine years, he'd pined after her, unable to recapture his usual zest for life. That kind of love and desire frightened Laurel and she'd wanted no part of it—until now.

She hadn't done much to make Edward want her. And maybe he just wasn't attracted to her in that way. She groaned softly. Suddenly, Sean had awakened all these strange and powerful feelings inside of her and she didn't know what to do with them. For the first time in her life, she felt real desire for a man.

From beneath the pillow, she heard the bedroom door open, then creak as it swung shut. She sat up, clutching the pillow to her lap. "You're back," she said.

In the faint light streaming through the window, she saw him turn toward the bed. "You're awake."

Laurel reached over and switched on the light, then hastily ran her fingers through her tousled hair. "I can't sleep. It's probably jet lag. It's afternoon in Hawaii."

Sean set a bottle of beer on the table near the sofa and slowly drew his sweater over his head. After he'd tossed it aside, he sat and kicked off his shoes and socks. "You've had a busy day."

She nodded. "You were talking to Alistair." At his questioning look, Laurel smiled. "I went looking for you. What were you talking about?"

"Nothing," Sean said.

"I—I thought you'd left. For good."

"We have a deal. I'm not going to back out," Sean said.

Laurel caught herself staring at his chest and when she looked back at his face, he was watching her. "I—I wouldn't blame you if you wanted out. This is a pretty crazy plan."

"It is." He reached for the buttons on his jeans and she scrambled for the light and turned it off. It took a moment for her eyes to adjust again, and by the time they had, he wore only his boxers. Laurel swallowed hard. Maybe she hadn't felt this kind of attraction to Edward because he didn't have the body of a Greek god.

He sat on the sofa, bracing his elbows on his knees. "Maybe you should tell me why this money is so important to you."

"There are things I want to do with my life," she murmured. "And I want to get started now."

"Like what?" he asked as he rose. Sean moved to the bed and sat on the edge. Her pulse quickened as the mattress sank under his weight. "Tell me."

She could barely see him in the dark, but she felt the heat from his body, heard the soft sound of his breathing. He found her hand and slipped his fingers between hers, drawing it up to his mouth.

"I—I have this plan," she said as he pressed a kiss to the tip of one finger. "I'm going to do something good with the money. But I can't talk about it. I'm afraid I'll jinx it."

"You can tell me, Laurel." Sean kissed another finger, his lips soft. She shivered, grateful that she didn't keep any really embarrassing secrets. No secret would be safe once Sean started kissing her. "I found this old building in a neighborhood in Dorchester and I want to open an arts center there. We'd have after-school activities in theater, music, dance, maybe painting." She reached over and turned on the light, suddenly excited to be telling someone about her plans. "You should see the building. It's perfect. It's got all this space and it's right on the bus line. And it's within walking distance of two grade schools."

"That's what you want the money for?"

Laurel nodded. "When I was little, my mother sent me to art lessons and dance class. And in the summer, she took me to acting classes. When she died, I could hardly think about that time in my life, because it was so much a part of my memories of her. It hurt too much. But then when I started teaching music, it all came back to me. Those teachers made a difference in my life."

"It's a great idea," Sean said.

She clutched his hand, pulling it to her. "Do you really think so?"

"Who knows? Something like that might have made a difference for me."

Laurel smiled. "I told you my secrets. Now you have to tell me yours."

"I don't have any secrets," Sean replied.

She took his hand and kissed his fingertips one by one. "I promise, I won't judge." He stared at her for a long moment and Laurel felt a shiver skitter down her spine. Sometimes he looked at her and she saw desire in his eyes, knew that if she just leaned forward, he'd kiss her. Was any of this real between them? Did he fantasize about her in the same way she did about him?

"All right," Sean said. "Shove over."

Laurel shimmied to the other side of the bed and Sean lay down beside her, stretching his long legs out in front of him. This nervous anticipation, the flutter of her heart when Sean moved beside her, the quickening of her pulse when his shoulder bumped against hers—all of it was so exciting.

He leaned back into the pillows and sighed. "My childhood wasn't the best. My da was a commercial fisherman and he was gone all the time. My ma walked out when I was three. And my brothers and I raised ourselves. I grew up...confused. And angry. And rebellious."

"Did you get in trouble?"

"I was well on my way to a career as a criminal."

"And what stopped you?"

Sean shrugged, a response that she'd grown used to already. He shrugged when he needed more time to think, always so careful about what he revealed, so wary of letting someone know him. He was a man of very few words and Laurel had grown to love that about him.

"There were a lot of petty little crimes. And then, one day, I stole a car and spent a night in jail. And I realized I was just one step away from losing control of my life. It took a while for that to sink in all the way. I got fired from a few jobs, got bounced out of the police academy. Then I took a few courses and got my P.I. license."

"And now you break up weddings for a living?" Laurel teased.

Sean chuckled. He didn't laugh often, but the sound was like a tiny victory for her. He trusted her enough to let her in, to show her a side that he didn't reveal often. She'd thought her childhood scars ran deep, but Sean's weren't even scars. The wounds still seemed raw.

"I think I did you a favor." He slipped his arm around her shoulders and pulled her against him.

Laurel's hand rested on his chest and she watched as it rose and fell with his breathing. "I think you did," she murmured. "I think you rescued me."

She stared at him, waiting, hoping, that he'd kiss her. And then he did, a sweet and gentle kiss, the warmth of his mouth sending a wave of wonderful sensation through her body. Laurel wondered if he knew the power he had over her, how just a simple kiss could make her lose all sense of who she was.

He pulled back and gently brushed her hair out of her eyes. "I think you need to sleep," he murmured.

She curled into him, resting her head in the curve of his arm. Suddenly exhaustion overwhelmed her and her eyes grew heavy. "I'm tired."

"I'll be here when you wake up," he said.

She felt his lips on her forehead and Laurel smiled. Maybe this "marriage" wouldn't be so bad after all. If she could just find a way to keep him in her bed, it might be better than she'd ever expected.

SEAN OPENED HIS EYES slowly and found himself in an unfamiliar bed. For a moment, he wasn't sure where he was. The thought that he'd had too much to drink the previous night drifted through his mind, but he didn't have a headache and his mouth didn't taste like a used gym sock. He slowly pushed up on his elbows and looked around the room.

"Laurel," he murmured before letting himself fall back into the pillow. He rolled over onto his stomach and closed his eyes. He'd never spent an entire night in a woman's bed. And what time he had spent had involved sex.

Even though they hadn't been intimate, the thought of making love to Laurel hadn't been far from his mind. But she'd said it herself—he'd rescued her. And if he wanted to avoid the Quinn family curse, then he needed to exercise some self-control.

The bathroom door swung open and Laurel stepped out. His face still pressed into the pillow, Sean watched her surreptitiously through one eye. She wore a robe made of loose, flowing fabric that gaped at her breasts and clung to her limbs.

She glanced over at the bed, but from her angle he must have appeared to be sleeping. A moment later, she let the robe drop to the floor, offering him a tempting view of her backside. He held his breath, afraid to move, and watched as she pulled a lacy bra and panties out of her wardrobe.

A groan nearly slipped from his throat as he let his gaze drift from the nape of her neck to her long legs. God, she had a beautiful body, curves in all the right places, and skin that had felt like silk beneath his hands.

His response to the sight of her naked form was involuntary and he felt himself grow hard. Sean knew he ought to look away, or to at least let her know he was watching. But he waited until she'd pulled on a sleeveless blouse and finished buttoning it before he moved. And when he did, she quickly turned.

"Good morning," Laurel said, hurrying to the closet to retrieve a short little flowered skirt. "Are you awake?"

As he sat up, Sean tried to act sleepier than he really was. In truth, his blood was racing so quickly through his veins and his heart was pounding so hard that he could have jumped out of bed and run five miles in record time. "I'm awake," he murmured. More awake than even he wanted to be.

"Get up," she said. "I want to take you somewhere." She crossed to the bed and sat on the edge, not bothering to finish dressing. Her long legs were bare and did nothing to alleviate his discomfort.

"Give me a moment," Sean said.

She grabbed his hand and gave it a tug, but he pulled back until she tumbled beside him onto the bed. He wanted to kiss her, to run his hands up and down her gorgeous legs. But Sean knew that doing so wouldn't help his...condition.

Laurel laughed, then sat beside him, crossing her legs in front of her. "I slept so well last night. I thought I'd be jet-lagged but I wasn't. I'm just full of energy. And I'm famished. I think we should go out and get some breakfast."

"I could use some coffee," Sean said. That, and a very cold shower. "Do you think Alistair made some?"

"I take it you're not a morning person?"

"Is it morning?"

"The sun is up. It's nearly nine. We have the whole day in front of us. Come on, we can get coffee on our way," she insisted. "Take a quick shower and then we can go."

Aw, hell. His reaction was only natural, a physiological response that most men experienced in the morning. He rolled off the bed and stood beside it. Her gaze skimmed along his chest, then stopped in the vicinity of his lap, at the obvious bulge in his boxers. Laurel cleared her throat and looked away.

"Maybe I'll go get you some coffee," she said. She quickly tugged on her skirt, then hurried to the door.

The door closed and Sean started toward the bathroom, hooking his thumbs in the waistband of the boxers and shoving them over his hips. But the door opened again and Sean froze. He glanced over his shoulder as she poked her head back inside.

"Oh, sorry," she murmured. She closed the door until it was open just a crack. "Sugar?" she asked, her voice a bit breathless.

"No."

Laurel closed the door behind her and Sean waited. Right on schedule, she opened the door again. If he didn't know Laurel, he might think she was deliberately trying to get a good look at his ass.

"Cream?" she asked.

"A little milk," he said.

When she'd closed the door again, Sean chuckled softly. Considering the effect his naked body had on her, maybe it would be best to walk around this way all the time. She'd certainly keep her distance.

He grabbed his toothbrush from his duffel, then walked to the bathroom. But he stopped a few steps inside and sighed. The room was almost as large as his bedroom at home. A huge tub stood against one wall, and nearby, a spacious shower. The vanity, littered with cosmetics and lotions and pretty bottles of perfume, had two sinks with shiny gold fixtures. Hell, even the toilet looked high-class.

Sean reached inside the shower and turned on the water. Immediately the scent of Laurel's shampoo filled the room. He quickly brushed his teeth, then stepped into the marble-lined stall. A low moan slipped from his throat as he stood beneath the rush of water.

The shower was like everything else in the mansion, functional but in a very luxurious way. He tipped his head back and ran his fingers though his hair, then grabbed a bar of soap in lieu of shampoo. He didn't want to spend the day smelling like Laurel. He had enough trouble keeping his mind—and his hands—off of her.

The shower was too relaxing to leave and he stayed beneath the water until his fingers began to wrinkle. The bathroom was filled with steam as he stepped out and wrapped a plush towel around his waist. When he walked out of the bathroom, he found Laurel waiting, sitting on the bed with a tray filled with food.

"Alistair made us breakfast in bed," she said. "He thinks we're still on our honeymoon."

The impulse to tell her that Alistair knew the truth about their "marriage" was immediate, but he decided against revealing the secret for now. He'd save that news for another time. He wanted the charade to continue a little longer—just to see where it would lead.

Sean readjusted the towel, wondering what would happen if he just let it drop to the floor. Would she run? Or would she pull him onto the bed and explore his body with her hands. He pushed the thoughts aside, unwilling to let himself become aroused again.

He pulled a silver cover off a plate. "French toast."

Laurel pointed to another covered plate as she munched on a croissant. "An egg-white omelette with tomatoes and green peppers. My favorite." She pulled up another cover. "And I don't know who would eat all this for breakfast. Fried eggs, fried mushrooms, fried tomato, bacon, sausage, some kind of potato pancake and canned beans." She winced. "This is a heart attack waiting to happen. I'm surprised Alistair didn't fry the napkin and silverware while he was at it."

Sean grinned. Leave it to Alistair. The man certainly knew how to please. "That's an Irish breakfast," he said. "Everything but the black-and-white pudding."

"Irish people eat pudding for breakfast?"

"Black-and-white pudding is two kinds of sausage made of—" He paused. "Never mind."

She frowned as she stared down at the plate. "Why would Alistair make you—"

"He probably thought I'd enjoy a hearty breakfast. Maybe this is what he eats for breakfast."

She seemed satisfied with the answer and poured herself a cup of coffee.

"There is one thing I'd like," he said.

"What is it? I'll call Alistair. He'll make you whatever you want."

Sean reached out and hooked his finger beneath her chin, then turned her face to his. "This is what I want," he said, leaning forward. He covered her mouth with his, tasting the strawberry jam that she'd smeared on the croissant. He didn't pull back right away, instead lingering, testing and tasting until he was satisfied that he'd sated that particular hunger.

He'd been fighting his impulses for far too long. And now that he'd given in and admitted this powerful attraction he had to Laurel, Sean realized that he'd been silly to deny himself. Just because they kissed and touched, didn't mean that the curse was working. He was just following his natural instincts. Laurel was a beautiful woman, he was a healthy man. And when it came time to walk away, he'd do it.

Turning back to his breakfast, Sean grabbed a fork and speared a crispy brown sausage. "A great way to start the day," he murmured.

"The food?" she asked, her expression still a bit startled.

"No, the kiss." He sent her a grin. "The food is good, too."

As they enjoyed their breakfast, Sean decided that he could get used to a life of luxury. He was making a decent wage and spending time with a beautiful woman. And Alistair was a helluva good cook. Life couldn't get much better.

But as he watched Laurel wrap her kiss-swollen lips around a forkful of omelette, he realized that life *could* get a whole lot better—and a whole lot more complicated in the process.

5

DUST MOTES SWIRLED in the air as Sean and Laurel walked through the old storefront. Tall windows, covered with a wire mesh outside, were cracked and broken and grimy with dirt—a sign that the building had been vacant for some time. And with outside temperatures nearing eighty, the air inside was stale and musty, heavy with the heat of the early September afternoon.

"What do you think?" Laurel asked.

Sean glanced around. She'd been so excited to show him this place, he was afraid to admit that he'd expected something a little nicer. "I think you have a lot of work to do."

"I know," she said, excitement filling her voice. "But I think it would make a great children's center. And I can probably get some matching grants from local foundations and maybe even from the government to do the renovations. The first thing I'm going to do is hire someone who is really good at fund-raising. Five million won't last long if we don't bring money in."

"What if your uncle doesn't give you the five million?"

"I'm thinking positively. He has to give me the money," she said, a desperate edge invading her cheerful voice. "I can't lose this place. It's too perfect."

Sean didn't see it as perfect. In truth, it was about as far from perfect as a building could get. But he couldn't deny Laurel's enthusiasm. "How can you be so sure this is what you want to do?"

Laurel slowly turned, taking in the entire room. "I just am. It's as if my past is connected now with my present. There were times when I felt like I was...drifting. When my father died, my last tether to who I was, was cut. This place makes me feel like I have my feet back on the ground."

"It must be nice to be sure," Sean said.

"Aren't you?"

In truth Sean had never been sure of anything in his life. He'd always waited for the next bad thing to happen, for the next disaster to come knocking at the door. There was only one person he could truly trust and depend on in the world—himself. "Yeah," he lied.

"I'm going to name this place the Louise Carpenter Rand Center for the Arts," she said. "After my mother."

"What if your uncle asks for proof before he hands over the money? What if he wants to see a marriage certificate?"

"I'll deal with that then," she said. "My father never realized what it would be like for me, living under Sinclair's thumb. If he'd known, he wouldn't have put my uncle in charge of my trust. And if he were alive, I know he'd support this idea. My mother would have loved it, too. I'm thinking positively." She turned to face the room. "Now, this is going to be the dance studio. We'll put mirrors on that wall and put in a new floor." She did a fancy little ballet step around him.

"And over here, I'd like to have an art studio. And behind that wall would be storage for materials and supplies. And downstairs in the front part of the building, I want a small gallery and performance space, so people in the neighborhood can visit and see what we're doing here."

She danced by and Sean grabbed her around the waist and stopped her. "You could talk to Sinclair about your idea, lay out your plan. He might decide to support it."

"You don't know him," she said, shaking her head. "He formed his ideas about the opposite sex back in the Neanderthal ages. He thinks the only future for me is marriage and children and a nice little three-bedroom cave. His idea of the perfect husband has nothing at all to do with love. If the guy can keep track of my money, then he's a perfect candidate."

He stared down into her gaze and Laurel grew still. "Did you love Eddie?" Sean asked. He didn't want to know the answer, but he had to.

"Edward," she corrected. Laurel considered his question for a moment. "No. But he was the only one asking me to marry him. And I thought he was the kind of man I could live with. That was enough for me."

"You sell yourself short," Sean said. He released her and walked across the room to examine a broken door. Why couldn't she see how wonderful she was? She was beautiful and sexy and smart, and the kind of woman any man would want. Why would she settle for a guy like Eddie the Cruiser?

Laurel followed him. "And how would you know?

Do you think I should give up my dreams while I wait for a man to ride to my rescue? I want to do something with my life. I want to make a difference, and I can't do that if Sinclair won't give me my money."

"Find it somewhere else," he said, his voice tight.

"Who is going to give me five million dollars?"

"Like you said. Foundations. The government. Have you tried?"

Anger suffused her expression. "You don't think I can do this, do you? You're just like Uncle Sinclair!"

"Laurel, that's not true. I'm just—"

A sudden movement above their head startled Laurel and she screamed as a pigeon swooped in between them. A moment later she was in his arms, her breath coming in tiny gasps.

"It's just a pigeon," he murmured, smoothing his hand over her hair and watching the bird perch on a pipe near the ceiling. He distractedly tucked a strand behind her ear then ran his palm along her jaw.

Sean waited for her to pull away, to break the intimate contact. But her gaze was fixed to his mouth. His thumb found her lower lip and he dragged it across, watching as she closed her eyes and turned into his touch.

She looked like an angel, the sun streaming through a window behind her and bathing her pale hair in an unearthly light. He bent closer and touched his mouth to hers and she instantly responded, opening to his kiss. It was like touching heaven and tasting immortality. Every ounce of his being was focused on the feel of her lips beneath his.

A kiss had always been something very simple to

him, an enjoyable pastime and a necessary step in seduction. But with Laurel the experience was like nothing he'd ever felt before. They seemed to communicate with the touch of their tongues and the soft shift of their lips.

It was everything he needed, but it wasn't enough. Sean wrapped his arms around her waist and picked her up, never breaking contact with her mouth. He wasn't sure where he was going, but when he found a rough brick wall, he gently trapped her there, pulling her legs up around his waist.

The kiss turned more desperate and Laurel pushed her palms beneath his T-shirt, shoving it up around his chest. The feel of her hands on his skin was electric, sending a current racing through his body and setting his nerves on fire. He couldn't stop himself, even if he wanted to. He couldn't.

With one arm wrapped firmly around her waist, Sean worked at the buttons of her blouse, shoving the fabric aside until he could press his mouth to her shoulder. Her skirt was gathered around her hips and his hands skimmed over her legs, still wrapped around his waist.

Of all the places for desire to overwhelm them, this had to be the worst choice. The temperature in the building felt close to one hundred degrees and there was nowhere comfortable to continue this seduction. If he let it go further, there would be no turning back— because he wanted to make love to Laurel, to experience her body in the same way he enjoyed her mouth.

He slid his hand from her shoulder down to her breast, cupping the soft flesh in his palm. He'd always been so uneasy with women, not when it came to seduction, but with what came after—the emotion and the intimacy. Sex had been about satisfying a need. With Laurel, Sean knew it would be more.

Just the thought of stripping off their clothes and letting their desires overwhelm them caused his heart to hammer and his blood to warm. His arousal was powerful, and anticipation raced though him each time he shifted her in his embrace.

The sound of wings flapping above their heads caused Laurel to suck in a sharp breath and Sean used the chance to gather his control. He wanted her, more than he'd ever wanted a woman before. Yet not here, and not now. But *soon*. "We should go," he murmured.

She froze, her breath stilling. Sean glanced up to see confusion fill her eyes. To reassure her, he kissed her again, gently yet thoroughly, making it clear that there would be more to come another time. Then he let her body slide down along his, stifling a groan as she rubbed against his arousal.

"I guess we really don't have to practice that part of marriage," she said.

Sean worked at the buttons of her blouse. "Practice makes perfect."

She sighed and reached up to touch his cheek. "Yes, it does."

As they restored order to their clothes, the intimacy didn't stop. Laurel smoothed her hands over his chest, then brushed his hair out of his eyes. And Sean took a last chance to touch her, raking his fingers through her hair and pulling it back from her face.

It was as if they both knew the inevitable was coming. They would make love and it would be perfect between them. But when and where would be decided later.

THE NIGHT was as warm and humid as the day had been, summer holding tight to the first weeks of September. Laurel slowly strolled along the stone terrace that overlooked the swimming pool. It was the one luxury she gave into, insisting that if she had to live in the mansion, Sinclair would have to pay for a pool man.

Sinclair preferred the family vacation home in Maine, a rough lodge on Deer Island. There, he could focus all his attention on his coins, his stamps and his other obsessions. He had so many things to occupy his time, why did he continue to interfere in her life? Even the house had become a source of contention between them. The mansion was half hers—the half that her father had left her. But Sinclair owned the other half and neither one of them could sell unless the other agreed.

Laurel sat on the low wall that surrounded the terrace. There were times when the mansion seemed like such a burden, another chain tying her to her uncle. But she felt differently now—now that Sean was living here with her. She turned and glanced back at the tall windows of the dining room, illuminated in the dusk by the crystal chandelier that her father had bought in Paris.

Her thoughts focused on the man she'd brought home as her "husband," the man who was sitting with her uncle in the library, pouring over the old man's stamp collection. A tiny shiver skittered down her spine. After their encounter earlier that morning, they'd both tried to act as if nothing had happened. But with each kiss and each caress they shared, she and Sean were moving closer and closer to total surrender.

She turned back to stare out at the lawn, the swallows diving across the grassy width from their nests in the old carriage house. The air was growing thick with the sounds of evening, crickets and night birds, while bees still buzzed in the flowers. Laurel closed her eyes and took in a deep breath. She could have him if she really wanted him. All she had to do was to make the first move and to keep moving until he couldn't stop.

But so much of her life had been about following her whims and impulses. She'd never learned to think before she acted. Yes, she and Sean might have a wonderful night together, maybe even ten or twenty wonderful nights. But if she didn't look before she leaped this time, she might hit bottom and seriously hurt herself.

"What are you doing out here?"

Laurel didn't bother turning around. Sean slipped his hands around her waist and pulled her against his chest. His palms moved down to her hips and he nuzzled her neck. "I'm enjoying the silence," she said.

"We just finished a discussion about my choice of neckwear," Sean said. He grabbed the tie and flipped it over her shoulder. "I like the design. Sinclair thinks the only appropriate pattern for a man is stripes. I think he was questioning my masculinity."

"Well, I can vouch for your masculinity," she said, turning in his arms. Her thoughts returned to that morning, when he'd been unable to hide his arousal—and she'd been unable to hide her curiosity. An image of his naked backside flashed in her mind, causing her pulse to quicken. He was quite beautiful...in a purely masculine way.

"And I like the tie," Sean said.

"It is nice," she said, fingering the silk. "So you forgive me for putting you through an afternoon of shopping?"

After they'd visited the old storefront in Dorchester, Laurel had insisted that they stop at Louis Boston and Brooks Brothers to pick up some new clothes for Sean. He had grumbled at first, but when he'd seen how much she was enjoying herself, he'd relaxed and played male model for her.

"The clothes make me look respectable."

He did look so sophisticated and sexy in his new clothes. The finely cut shirt hugged his torso and accented his narrow waist, and the trousers fit his backside perfectly. "And I was just missing your regular clothes," Laurel said. "They make you look...dangerous."

There was something about Sean Quinn, beyond the T-shirts and jeans, that made him seem that way. When she'd first met him, he'd been distant and aloof. But he'd begun to drop his defenses and let her peek behind the walls. One moment he'd be cool and indifferent, and then, suddenly, he'd reveal a sweet, tender and oddly vulnerable man. And with every minute they spent together, she chipped a bit more of the wall away and—

Laurel pushed the thought from her head. No, she wasn't falling in love with him! Maybe she was infatuated or captivated or caught up in the passion of the moment. But she couldn't allow herself to believe this was a real marriage or even a relationship. It was a business arrangement and nothing more.

Tipping her face up, he forced her gaze to meet his, then brushed a kiss across her lips. "Your uncle wants me to look at a new stamp," he said. "He's waiting for me in the library."

"Sinclair will have you in there all night long. Stay here with me. We're 'newlyweds.' Sinclair will have to understand." She wrapped her arms around his neck and teased at his mouth, tempting him with another quick taste before pulling away.

Sean groaned and dragged her into a deeper kiss, his tongue invading her mouth. At first she thought he would stop there, but he didn't. His hands gently explored her body. He sat on the low wall and pulled her between his legs, pushing her top up so he could kiss her belly.

Laurel sighed and gave herself over to the overwhelming need racing through her body, grabbing his hands and sliding them higher until they rested just below her breasts. "Take me to bed," she urged, furrowing her hands through his hair.

"I can't," he whispered.

The heat racing through her suddenly dissolved, replaced by a chill that caused every muscle in her body to tense. "You can't?"

"Sinclair is waiting for me," he said, trailing kisses from her bellybutton to her hip. "The sooner we convince your uncle that I'm the perfect husband, the sooner you'll get your five million. You have to let me do my job."

She cursed inwardly. Right now she didn't give a

damn about the money! All that mattered was the way he made her feel when he touched her. "You don't have to do all this."

He quickly stood and gave her one last kiss. "I want to, Laurel. It's for a good cause."

A shiver jolted her body and she rubbed her bare arms as she watched him walk back into the house. Could she have made her needs any clearer? He wanted her, but only up to a point. Maybe he just didn't find her sexy enough.

Well, she'd find out for sure soon enough. In an hour or two, they'd be alone in her bedroom. If she really wanted him, she could make her move then.

But was she ready to risk her heart for a night of passion—or risk her pride on the chance that he might refuse her? Laurel took a ragged breath and closed her eyes. If any man was worth the gamble, it was Sean Quinn.

As she walked up the stairs, she heard Sinclair's voice droning on and on in the library. For a moment, she thought about rescuing Sean and dragging him upstairs with her. But instead, she ran up the stairs to her room and closed the door behind her. She felt as if her body were on fire, the anticipation so acute it was almost painful.

Leaving a trail of clothes behind her, she walked to the bathroom and turned on the shower, making sure the temperature was colder than comfortable. Laurel stepped inside and let the water pour over her, washing away the heat of the day and the flush of desire that he'd cast over her body.

But even though her skin prickled with goose

bumps, the ache refused to abate. She turned up the hot water and let it pound on her back, hoping it might relax her. Bracing her arms on the marble wall, Laurel tried to clear her mind. A sound behind her caused her to turn and she saw a shadow on the other side of the shower door.

From the outline of the figure, the width of the shoulders and the long legs, she knew it was Sean. She held her breath, waiting, wondering what she should do. He reached for the door, then pulled his hand away. He was turning to leave when Laurel reached out for the handle and pushed it open.

She knew the move was impulsive but she didn't regret it. Had she really thought about her choice, she may have stayed in the shower alone, but she wasn't about to throw away what could be her only chance. The steam swirled out behind her and a tremor of anticipation raced through her. "I thought you were going to stay downstairs with Sinclair."

"I told him I was tired," Sean murmured, his gaze skimming over her naked body like a caress.

"Are you?"

He shook his head and glanced at the door. "If you want me to leave you alone, I will."

Her knees went weak. "I don't want you to go." She took a step toward him and he took it as an invitation.

Sean kicked off his shoes, then stepped into the shower with her, fully clothed. He pulled the door shut behind him, and in an instant, his hands were on her body and his mouth covered hers. It was as if they'd stepped into a dream, the shower stall refilling with steam, the passion like a wave washing over them.

She tugged at his clothes, but it was difficult to unbutton his shirt when it was wet. With a low groan, Sean removed his necktie and then tore off his shirt, the buttons pinging against the marble walls of the shower. There wasn't much space inside, their bodies pressed together as the water streamed over them.

When his shirt hit the floor of the shower, Laurel smoothed her hands over his chest. Every time she touched him, it was like touching him for the first time. Her fingers mapped his body, learning every inch of flesh, smooth skin and hard muscle. Sean tipped his head back and closed his eyes as her mouth replaced her hands on his chest.

She hadn't realized until this moment how much she wanted him. Suddenly she couldn't think straight, her brain focused not on rational thought but on the wild sensations racing though her body. As she undid his belt, her hand brushed against his groin and she found him hard and fully aroused, his erection evident through the wet fabric of his trousers.

With a hesitant hand, she touched him there and a low groan slipped from his throat. He braced his hands on the sides of the shower as she worked on his zipper. Laurel held her breath, hooked her fingers into the waistband of his trousers, and slowly pulled down, stripping away his boxers at the same time and leaving them at his feet.

As she worked her way back up, she explored his long legs with her hands. He was beautifully formed, an image of masculine perfection. She'd never known a man's body to be so tempting, every inch a promise of the passion to come. Suddenly it all became so fascinating.

Laurel ran her fingers along his shaft and delighted at his reaction, the sharp breath he sucked in, the quiver of his belly. But when she pressed her lips to his heat, Laurel realized her power over him, how completely vulnerable he was to her touch. He whispered her name and furrowed his fingers through her wet hair when she took him into her mouth.

As she caressed him with her hands and her lips, she sensed his usual reticence dissolve and he opened his soul to her. Laurel had never felt so close to a man before, so anxious to please and so desperate to possess. She'd wondered about her true feelings for Sean and now she had no doubts. This was no longer a business relationship, this was heat and desire and need, so strong that it frightened her.

She brought him close to his release and then pulled back, but Sean had other plans for her. He took her arms and pulled her up in front of him, then kissed her, his lips ravaging hers. He pressed her body against the wall of the shower, trapping her in his embrace, his mouth plundering and demanding, then moving along her shoulder to her breast and then her nipple.

A shudder raced through Laurel's body, and when his fingers found the spot between her legs, she cried out in surprise at the jolt that followed. She had imagined what it might be like between them, but she'd envisioned a seduction more traditional—a bed, the judicious removal of clothing, and then a slow, easy stroll toward release. But this was frantic and wild, uncontrolled to the point that she couldn't think. Every moment was marked by new pleasures and a need that twisted her to the core.

"What are you doing to me?" he murmured, his lips warm on her breast. "Why do I want you so much?"

He plunged his fingers inside her and she cried out, nearly reaching her pleasure right then. But Sean slowed himself, his breath coming in deep gasps, his body tensed and waiting. He bent to retrieve his wallet from the pocket of his pants.

Laurel smiled as he dumped out the wet contents and found a foil package. It took only a moment for her to sheath him and then he was inside her, their joining more powerful and desperate than anything she'd experienced in her life. He pulled her legs up around his hips as he drove into her, each stroke taking her closer to the edge.

Soon she lost all sense of time and reality, the water splashing around them and the steam filling her lungs. Laurel ran her fingers through his hair and watched his face as he made love to her, marveling at the exquisite mix of pleasure and pain suffusing his features, the concentration that seemed to propel him forward and at the same time hold him back.

As if he could sense her watching him, he opened his eyes and their gazes locked. He slowed his movements, pulling out much farther before plunging back inside her. Laurel sensed that he was waiting for her. She shifted over him and a wave of pleasure raced through her.

He saw it in her face and, a moment later, they were at the edge together. His mouth covered hers as he came, his shoulder muscles going tense before he exploded inside her. He moaned, murmured her name, and then she joined him, tumbling through ecstasy, held tight in his arms.

Gradually, reality returned and Laurel felt the water on her skin and the marble on her back. She nuzzled her face into his neck and waited for her breathing to return to normal. Completely sated, she was afraid to put her feet back on the floor, afraid that she couldn't stand on her own.

Sean reached over and turned off the water, then kicked open the door, still buried deep inside her. As he carried her to the bed, dripping water along the way, he kissed her softly. "We should make it a habit to shower together every day," he said.

"To conserve water," she said.

He chuckled as he laid her on the bed, his body stretching out on top of hers. Laurel ran her hand across his cheek. When Sean smiled, she felt as if anything was possible, as if there would be many showers that ended in many more evenings like this. Maybe that was a dream or a fantasy or wishful thinking. But for now, she wasn't going to question her good fortune. She was simply going to enjoy it.

SEAN OPENED HIS EYES to the morning sun streaming through the bedroom window. Pushing up on his elbows, he glanced at Laurel, curled up beside him. Her hair, a riot of honey-colored waves, fell over her face. He brushed the curls back and kissed her cheek.

Her eyes fluttered and she looked up at him, a sleepy smile touching her lips. They'd only slept for three or four hours, but he didn't miss the rest. Losing himself in Laurel's body all night long had both exhausted and exhilarated him. He smiled at her as he stroked her cheek. "Morning."

"Is it? Or is it afternoon?"

"It's just past nine. God, you look pretty."

Laurel groaned and covered her face. Her fingers went to her hair and she groaned even louder.

Sean grabbed her hands and pinned them above her head. "I'm not kidding. You do look beautiful."

Her expression turned serious. "About last night, I—"

He dropped a kiss on her lips. "What about last night?"

"We share a bedroom," she said, "and we pretend to be husband and wife. But that wasn't about pretending last night, right?"

"I wasn't faking anything," Sean said, his expression serious. "Were you?"

A pretty blush stained her cheeks and she burrowed her face into his shoulder. "No, it was all very real...and wonderful." She looked up at him. "Do you have any regrets?"

Sean pressed his lips to her forehead. "No."

To his surprise, he realized he was telling the truth. He'd never in his life made love to a woman without regrets. The morning after had always been uncomfortable for him, especially since he didn't allow himself to hang around that long. Going in, he'd always known there wasn't a chance for a real relationship, and that had always caused an uneasy guilt the day after.

But with Laurel he felt nothing but utter contentment. He could imagine a relationship with her, going out to movies and dinner, spending quiet nights at home watching a ball game, waking up in each other's arms and making love all night long.

Everything he'd been avoiding for so long had now come to pass. He'd played the Mighty Quinn and he'd lost his heart. But oddly, it didn't feel like a loss. There wasn't an empty space where his heart had once been. Instead, when he was with Laurel, he felt as if his heart were growing, breaking the shell that had protected it for so long.

"I'll go get us some breakfast. You stay in bed."

"Toast," she murmured. "And coffee. No Irish breakfast."

He bent and kissed her cheek. "Toast and coffee."

Sean tugged on his jeans, not bothering with boxers, then grabbed a shirt. He glanced over at Laurel as she closed her eyes again, her hand curled near her face.

Maybe he shouldn't have stepped into that shower last night, but an irresistible force had drawn him there, a force he couldn't deny any longer. Since the first time he'd kissed her, Sean had known it would come to this. There was something about Laurel that made him forget all his fears. With her, he felt both safe and completely out of control, two feelings that he'd never really experienced before.

Here he was a thirty-year-old man, and he'd never allowed himself to get close to any woman he'd ever known. He'd never had a real relationship—at least nothing that involved mutual trust and honest emotion. Until now. With Laurel, it was real.

Sean sighed as he stopped at the top of the stairs.

Hell, he should know what was going on. The Quinn family curse had struck again. He'd rescued Laurel from a marriage to a con man and another Quinn had fallen victim. Yet now that he had, it didn't really bother him. Spending time with Laurel made him feel good...happy.

As he walked down the stairs, he heard the doorbell ring. "I'll get it, Alistair," he called. He didn't hear a reply from the butler so he continued to the door. When he found Eddie Perkins waiting on the other side, he regretted ever heeding the bell.

"What the hell are you doing here?" Sean demanded.

Eddie frowned. "Do I know you?"

Sean stepped out of the house and closed the door behind him. "You don't remember me?"

Eddie shook his head slowly, then stopped. "Oh, yeah. You're that guy. The one who was there when they arrested me. I asked you to—" Suddenly the significance of Sean's presence hit him. "Hey, what the hell are *you* doing here?"

"I'm here to keep you away from Laurel," Sean muttered. "Why aren't you in jail?"

"I was," Eddie said. "My second wife posted bail. She has a very forgiving nature."

"Get out of here," Sean warned. "If I see you around Laurel again, I'll beat the crap out of you."

"I have every right to see her. She's still my fiancée."

"She *was* your fiancée," Sean reminded him.

"Missing our wedding wasn't my choice. And I want to make it up to her. We were in love once and I think we could be again."

"She never loved you. Believe me. And believe this: I'm going to do whatever it takes to protect her from scum like you."

"Hey, I can understand. You've got a mark here with a boatload of money. There aren't many pigeons as beautiful as Laurel Rand out there, waiting to be plucked. But remember who introduced you. The least you could do is spread the wealth."

"Would you like me to hit you now or would you like a running start?"

Eddie held up his hands. "You think about it. I don't want to make trouble. I just want my fair share of the pie." With that, he turned around and hopped into the Benz convertible that was parked in the drive. "Tell Laurel I'll be back."

Sean cursed softly. The last thing he—or Laurel—needed right now was another visit from Eddie Perkins. If he decided to cause trouble, then this whole charade would be over more quickly than either he or Laurel wanted. He turned and walked back into the house. Alistair stood in the middle of the doorway. "Who was at the door?"

"No one," Sean said. "Wrong address."

Alistair regarded him with a suspicious look, his eyebrow arched. "Are you and Miss Laurel ready for breakfast? I can put something out for you in the breakfast room. Perhaps an Irish breakfast?"

"We'll be down in fifteen minutes," Sean said. He took the stairs two at a time. When he slipped back into Laurel's room, he found her still curled up beneath the covers. He crawled across the bed and tugged at the comforter. "Laurel. Are you awake?"

"I am now," she murmured.

"Eddie was just here."

Laurel rubbed her eyes and sighed. "Eddie who?"

"Edward. The man you were supposed to marry."

The sleepy expression faded from her face as she sprung upright. "Eddie was here?"

"Don't worry. No one saw him. I answered the door and he was there. He says he wants to talk to you. He says he still loves you." Sean watched her face for a reaction. "Do you still love him?"

"No!" Laurel cried. "I told you, I never did."

"Then you were marrying him just for the money?"

She took a moment before she shrugged. "We were compatible. At least, I thought we were. I didn't realize he was a bigamist or a con man. And I needed to get married. What do you think he wants?"

"You. And your money," Sean said.

"He could cause problems. What if Sinclair finds out?"

"Maybe it's time to talk to your uncle. To tell him the truth. We can't keep this up forever. He's bound to find out."

She crawled out of bed and grabbed her robe, draping it over her naked body. His gaze fell to the spot where the front gaped open, revealing the soft swell of her breast, a breast he'd enjoyed just the previous night. "I—I don't want to tell him. Not now. Not yet."

"Eddie isn't going away. I know guys like him. He'll be back."

"I can deal with Edward," she said.

Sean cursed softly. "I don't want you to deal with him."

Laurel slowly turned and stared at him, her mouth agape. "I don't believe you just said that. *You* don't want *me* to deal with him? You sound just like a husband. You know, I've taken care of myself for seven years now and I've done a pretty good job."

Her mood had changed so quickly, he couldn't adjust. "Oh, right," Sean snapped. "You were about to marry a bigamist until he got arrested. Then you hired me to step in for the groom to help you scam your uncle out of five million."

Her jaw went tight and she crossed her arms beneath her breasts. "I am not trying to scam him."

Sean shrugged. "Then what are you doing, Laurel?"

"What I'm doing is none of your business. You're getting paid to do a job and to keep your mouth shut. If you can't do that, then maybe you ought to leave now." She stalked to the door and yanked it open, only to find Alistair waiting on the other side.

"Breakfast," he said in a cheery voice.

"I'm not hungry," Laurel muttered. She slipped past him, leaving the butler to gaze at Sean in confusion.

"A little tiff, I presume?" he asked.

Sean shook his head. "I don't know what I said. But she's definitely mad."

Alistair strolled into the room and placed the breakfast tray on the bed. "Would you care for a bit of advice?"

Sean moved to the edge of the bed and raked his hands through his hair. "Yeah, I guess so."

"Give Miss Laurel a few hours to cool down. She can be a very determined woman and when she has her mind set on something, she doesn't let anything get in her way, including her impulsive nature. Or a crusty old gentleman who cares more about his stamps than his niece. Or a handsome young man pretending to be her husband."

Sean smiled and nodded. "Thanks, Alistair." He picked up the silver cover on one of the plates and inhaled the scent of another Irish breakfast. "If I ever get rich, I'm going to hire a butler just like you. I don't know how I ever got along without you."

Alistair nodded, clearly pleased by the compliment. "Thank you, sir."

6

THE SUN WAS HIGH in the sky and the weather warm. Laurel stood at the deep end of the pool and stared into the sparkling water, then sucked in a deep breath. She pushed off the edge and dove cleanly into the water, then stroked toward the shallow end. After two laps, she flipped over onto her back and stared up at the sky.

Her mind rewound to the argument she'd had with Sean earlier that morning. It had been so silly and petty. Maybe she'd been a little tired or felt a little vulnerable, but whatever had caused her response didn't matter. She'd sounded shrewish and ungrateful.

By day, she and Sean were supposed to act like husband and wife. But last night, they'd become lovers. And though she'd paid him for the former, she was getting the later free. If they were lovers, then he had every right to question her motives.

From the start, Laurel knew the growing intimacy they shared was dangerous. The moment he'd stepped into the shower, they'd tossed aside inhibition and hesitation and indulged in a passion that possessed them both. And though she barely knew Sean, she knew enough to want him above anything else.

When he'd looked into her eyes as they'd made love, she'd seen something there—a man she was fast falling in love with. He was passionate and completely irresistible. He was sweet and strong and dependable, the qualities most women would choose in a husband. But he was also flawed, holding himself at a distance when he felt vulnerable.

Laurel knew a troubled childhood had left him wary and distrustful. But when they were together, all of that fell away and he became everything she'd never known she'd wanted. She kicked to the other end of the pool, then braced her arms on the edge.

Caught in some strange limbo, she found herself pulled between a make-believe life that made her happy and a real life that was growing increasingly more complicated. Uncle Sinclair still hadn't mentioned her trust fund, even though, to his eyes, she and "Edward" had been married for more than two weeks.

Still, Laurel hadn't made a point of bringing up the subject herself. She knew as soon as Sinclair turned the money over to her, her time with Sean would come to an end. She didn't want it to be over yet. Perhaps he didn't have a place in her future, but, for now, she needed him in her present—and that was enough.

Laurel kicked beneath the water and sank to the bottom of the pool. When she looked up through the water, she saw a figure standing next to the pool. Sean had left earlier without saying a word to her. He'd told Alistair he'd probably be back for lunch, but Laurel hadn't wanted to question the butler further. Anxious to make amends with her make-believe husband, she pushed off from the bottom of the pool and broke the surface of the water.

But Alistair stood at the edge of the water, holding a

stack of thick towels. "May I get you some lunch, Miss Laurel? It's past noon."

Laurel pulled herself up out of the pool and took one of the towels. "I thought I'd wait for Sean—" She paused, then quickly corrected herself. "Edward. I want to wait for Edward."

Alistair smiled. "Mr. Sean called and said he wouldn't be home for lunch. He needed to see his family."

She stared at him, her mouth agape. "You know?"

"There isn't much that goes on in this house that I don't know about," he said. "I know about your ex-fiancé, Edward, and I can't say that I'm upset that he's been arrested. And I know why you were so anxious to get married. I'm not one to offer an opinion about your personal life, but I like Mr. Sean. He's a very dependable man."

Laurel smiled hesitantly. "I like him, too."

"You seem very happy together."

"We are. I didn't expect to like him so much."

"I think he likes you, too," Alistair said.

"Did he tell you that?"

"He doesn't have to say it, Miss Laurel. Mr. Sean is a man of very few words. His actions do most of the talking."

"We had a fight this morning."

"I gathered that."

"It was stupid. I said some things that I didn't mean. I wish I could do something to make it up to him."

"I think he'll forgive you," Alistair said.

She took another towel from his hands and dried her hair, then sat at the edge of the pool. Laurel patted the concrete beside her. "Sit with me," she said. Alistair spread a towel at his feet and sat. "You have to take off your shoes and your socks."

"Miss, I don't think that would be proper."

Laurel rolled her eyes, then reached over and tugged off his gleaming black oxfords. Alistair removed his own socks and carefully rolled up his trousers.

"Put them in," she said, dangling her own legs into the water.

The butler did as she ordered and as soon as his feet dipped into the pool, he smiled. "Well, that's lovely," Alistair said. "Quite refreshing."

"Sinclair would have a fit if he saw you," Laurel teased. "He's such a fuddy-duddy sometimes."

"He loves you very much, Miss Laurel."

She froze. "Sean?"

"No, your uncle."

Laurel forced a laugh, embarrassed by her assumption. "He does not! He enjoys making my life as difficult as possible."

"He's afraid if he gives you the money, you'll leave and he'll never see you again."

"How do you know that?"

"I've worked in this house since before your mother came to live here twenty-seven years ago. I've kept my eyes open."

"And what have you seen?"

Alistair paused before he spoke, as if he was trying to decide how much he wanted to reveal. "I was there the night your father met your mother. Sinclair and Stewart were in New York, and the night before, Sinclair had gone to see a musical play in which your mother was appearing. He was so captivated by her performance, it was all he could talk about."

"Sinclair?" Laurel asked.

Alistair nodded. "The next night, he went back to the theater, only he brought Stewart with him for moral support. Sinclair was determined to introduce himself to your mother. They waited at the stage door and when she appeared, he stepped up and asked her to accompany them to dinner. And at that dinner, your mother fell head over heals in love—with your father."

"Poor Sinclair," Laurel murmured.

"I don't know that he ever stopped loving your mother. All the time she lived here with Stewart, after she gave birth to you, and after she died, Sinclair was always in love with her. But he couldn't say anything. It wouldn't have been proper or prudent."

"And that's why he doesn't like me," Laurel said. "Because I'm Stewart's daughter and—"

"Oh, no, not so," Alistair said. "I think you look so much like your mother that he sees her every time he looks at you. He sees the love he lost. That's why he both pushes you away and keeps you close."

Tears stung the corners of Laurel's eyes. "I thought he hated me," she murmured. "I guess I was wrong."

"If he knew I told you this, he would sack me without a second thought. But I thought it was time you understood why your uncle does what he does."

Laurel stared into the water, sunlight glinting off the surface, the tile mosaic creating a swirl of color below. "And will he ever understand why I do what I do?"

"Give him a chance, Miss Laurel. It may take time, but I believe he'll come around."

Laurel slipped her hands around Alistair's arm and gave it a hug. "Maybe I should go talk to Uncle Sinclair."

"I think you have other fences to mend first...with your husband."

"But if I explain to Uncle Sinclair and—"

"Oh, no," Alistair said, shaking his head. "In my opinion, I think it's best to keep all your options open. Your little charade might just work to your advantage."

Laurel frowned. If Uncle Sinclair truly loved her, then there had to be a way to convince him of her plans for her trust fund. Why would Alistair want her to continue her sham of a marriage? She pushed the question from her mind. Alistair was the only person in the world she could truly trust, so maybe it was best to listen.

"Mr. Sinclair and I are leaving this afternoon for New York," Alistair said. "Perhaps you could prepare a lovely dinner for your husband and smooth things out between you two."

"I'm not a very good cook," Laurel said.

"Ah, but I'm a very good instructor."

Laurel threw her arms around Alistair's neck. "And you're a good friend, too."

He blinked, his eyes growing misty. "Thank you, Miss Laurel. I'm touched."

She got to her feet and held out her hand to help him stand. "I think we better get started in the kitchen. This may be a long afternoon."

THE HOUSE on Beacon Street was bustling with activity when Sean arrived. His sister, Keely, and her husband,

Rafe, had been renovating it for the past month and planned to move in before Thanksgiving. Contractors' vans were parked on the narrow street and equipment and materials had been stacked on the sidewalk outside.

Sean stepped around an electrician who was running a wire to the porch light, and walked in the open door. He strolled through the large foyer and peered up the central staircase. Though the house wasn't as large as the Rand mansion, it promised to be equally luxurious. Rafe Kendrick wouldn't spare any expense for the home he planned to share with his wife and their new baby.

Keely had told the family about her pregnancy at the last get-together, an event that he hadn't attended. The family grapevine had worked well and he'd heard the news on a message that Liam had left on his voice mail. "Anyone home?" Sean called.

"Back here!"

Sean walked toward the rear of the house and found the kitchen. Keely stood in the center of the gutted room, staring at a row of tiles she'd laid out on the floor. He stood at her side and stared down at the tiles.

"What do you think?" she asked.

"Are you waiting for them to move?"

Keely giggled and gave him a playful slap. "I'm trying to choose. I need something that isn't too dark but isn't too light."

Sean slipped his arm around her shoulder, then kissed the top of her head. "Congratulations. Liam told me about the baby."

Keely looked up at him, as if surprised by his show of affection. She slipped her arm around his waist. "Thanks. We're pretty excited. Rafe is just obsessed with getting this house done. I want to take a little more time. There are so many choices to make. But he's determined we're going to bring the baby home to this house."

"It's going to be nice," he said.

"It will," Keely agreed. She pulled him over to the French doors that overlooked the backyard. "Why don't you take a look at the garden and I'll get us something to drink. I have to talk to you about something."

Sean opened the door and walked outside. The garden was tiny but beautiful, with an old maple shading the brick patio. A pretty iron table had been placed near a small fountain and he took a seat facing an overgrown flower bed. He couldn't help but wonder why Keely had been so insistent on seeing him. He had his answer a few seconds later.

"Hello, Sean."

He stiffened at the sound of his mother's voice, refusing to turn around. He should have known something was up. Keely was just too anxious to see him and too secretive about why. His jaw tightened and he tried to keep himself from getting up and walking away.

Fiona circled the table and stood in front of him, but he wouldn't look up. He felt a hand on his shoulder. "It's time for you two to talk," Keely said. "This can't go on any longer." She walked back into the house and closed the door.

Fiona set a tray on the table and poured him a glass

of pink lemonade. "I asked Keely to call you, so you mustn't blame her. May I sit down?"

"Suit yourself."

Fiona nodded, then took a spot across from him, folding her hands in front of her. "I've been waiting for this moment for such a long time."

Sean glanced at her. He was amazed at how little she'd changed over the years, how much she still looked like the woman in the photo he carried. She was beautiful, and Sean could only imagine how stunning she must have been on the day she married Seamus Quinn.

But he wasn't a stupid kid anymore and she wasn't his angel. She was the woman who had loved him and then walked away. The anger still burned deep inside of him. But one thing he'd noticed lately was that the fire had been fading. Somehow he'd come to realize that if he ever expected to move on with his life, he'd have to sort out his past. And confronting his mother was the first step.

"I know you're angry with me and I don't blame you," Fiona continued. "I walked out of your life and you aren't required to let me in just because I'm your mother."

"You weren't much of a mother," he murmured.

"I know. I made some very bad choices and I accept all the blame you're willing to heap on me. Heap away."

He sat silently for a long time, deciding whether to stay and talk, or whether to walk away. "Tell me why you left," Sean demanded. "Make me understand."

She seemed anxious to answer, sitting up straighter

and fixing her gaze on his face. "There were so many reasons and none of them a good excuse. I was worn down. Seamus was drinking and gambling and all we seemed to do was argue. When we came to America, we had such grand dreams. But as time passed, Seamus forgot those dreams. He wasn't able to give me all that he'd promised when he'd married me." Fiona paused. "And I think he was ashamed of himself."

"So you ran away?"

"I tried to make things better. I wanted him to quit fishing and find a job that would keep him home, but he refused. And when I found myself pregnant again, I decided I had to make a break, to show him how precarious it had become between us. I had to show him what he was risking. A few days turned into a week and then a month, and pretty soon it was impossible to come back."

"I know about the other man," Sean said.

She inhaled a sharp breath, a stunned expression on her face. Then she slowly nodded. "There was another man," Fiona admitted. "No one knew about him except your father."

"I knew," Sean said, anger coloring his voice. "And about twenty of Da's buddies at the pub knew. I heard him tell the story one night when he was drunk and didn't know I was listening. He said you'd had an affair."

"No, it was never that!" Fiona said. "He was a friend and I took advantage of his kindness. I told him my problems and he listened and that's all that happened. But he fell in love with me and wanted me to leave Seamus and make a life with him."

"And what about us?"

"He wanted me to bring you boys with me. But I couldn't do it. I couldn't marry him, so I had no choice but to leave Boston."

"God, Ma, it was the seventies. You could have gotten a divorce. We might have had a normal childhood."

"No, I couldn't get a divorce. I was, and still am, a good Catholic, and when I married your father, I married him for life. I knew if I stayed in Boston, I might break my wedding vows, so I left. I only meant to go for a short time. But the days passed and it never seemed to be the right time to return. Then after I was gone for too long, I was afraid your father wouldn't want me."

"And what about us?"

Fiona shook her head. "I never stopped loving you. And I never stopped loving your father. After all this, I still love him." A smile touched her lips. "He was such a charmer when we first met. From the moment I first saw him, I knew he was the one for me."

"How did you know?" Sean asked. He'd heard his brothers say the exact thing about the women in their lives and he'd felt the same way about Laurel. But the feelings didn't make sense to him. Maybe his mother could explain.

"There was magic in the air that day," she said. "It sounds silly, I know. Even though you don't remember Ireland, it's in your blood, Sean, and someday you'll feel it. You're a Quinn and the magic is always there. You just have to let yourself feel it." She took a sip of her lemonade and waited for his reply.

"I don't believe in magic," he murmured.

"Your father tells me that you got married."

Sean groaned inwardly. The family grapevine was still hard at work. "I'm not married. Just pretending to be."

"And why would you do that?" she asked.

"It's a very long story."

"Tell me about this woman. Is this someone you would like to marry?"

"I'm not the marrying kind," Sean said impatiently. Though he'd once believed the words, the sentiment now rang hollow. How did he know? Didn't he deserve the same happiness that his brothers and sister had found?

"You deserve to be loved," Fiona said, echoing Sean's thoughts. "Everyone deserves to be loved. It's the true joy of life. But if you don't believe in magic, then you'll never see it. Even if it's right in front of your nose." She reached out and covered his hand with hers.

Sean stared down at her fingers and a strange sense of déjà vu came over him. This was the first time she'd touched him since he'd been a very young child, and nothing had changed. Her touch still made him feel safe and warm. Emotion clogged his throat and, for a moment, speech was impossible. "Maybe we can talk again," he finally said, looking into her eyes.

"I'd like that," she said. "Very much."

SEAN PARKED Laurel's car in front of the mansion and stared up at the facade. Since his visit with Fiona, he'd been driving around aimlessly, trying to clear his head of some of the chaos inside. Until a few weeks ago, his life had been pretty simple. He worked, he ate, he slept.

But now he realized that he wasn't really living. He was existing, watching life from the sidelines, standing in a void of emotion. From the moment he'd walked down the aisle with Laurel, his life had been irrevocably changed. He suddenly had crucial choices to make and new emotions to deal with.

His thoughts returned to that morning, to the argument he'd had with Laurel, and then to the night before. Just the thought of her naked in his arms, arching against him in pleasure, sent a current of desire crackling through his body. But after a night made for fantasy, the morning had brought an odd reality. He was still doing a job and she was paying him to do it. And when she didn't need him anymore he'd be sent away. He'd leave much wealthier, but what would the experience cost him?

He walked to the front door and punched in the security code that opened it. The foyer was silent as he stepped inside. The scent of dinner drifted in the air and Sean quietly walked toward the kitchen. He pushed the door open, expecting to find Alistair there. But to his surprise he found Laurel, a kitchen towel wrapped around the waist of her sexy black dress.

Her back to him, she pulled the lid off a pot and peered inside, then picked up a piece of paper and read it out loud. "'The pasta goes in ten minutes before dinner is served,'" she murmured.

She picked up a glass of wine that sat on the counter

beside her and took a sip, then slowly turned, her gaze meeting his.

"Hi," Sean said.

"You're home," she countered, a smile touching the corners of her lips.

It was a nice illusion, that this was indeed his home. But Sean knew the truth. The home belonged to Laurel. He was no more than a visitor—or, like Alistair, an employee. "I'm home," he said.

"I've made dinner. We're having filet of beef, and pasta with a wild mushroom sauce. And a salad of spring greens. And for dessert, a rich chocolate mousse. I made it myself." A faint blush colored her cheeks. "Actually, Alistair helped."

"Where is Alistair?"

"He and Uncle Sinclair left for New York earlier this evening. The coin auction is tomorrow. So we're all alone."

"Laurel, I think we should—"

"Talk about this morning," she completed. "I want to apologize. I didn't mean to snap at you. I'm sorry, but with Eddie showing up and everything else going on, I just got a little overwhelmed."

"I shouldn't have voiced my opinion. It wasn't my place."

"No," Laurel cried, crossing the kitchen. She reached out and took his hand, and Sean felt his pulse leap at her touch. His mind flashed an image of the previous night, her naked body above his as they made love, her hair tumbled around her face, and the look of wonder in her eyes as she reached her release. He fought the impulse to yank her into his arms and to carry her up to the bedroom and make it all happen again. Now was not the time to give in to desire.

"Yes," he said. "I'm doing a job here."

"Is that what it is to you?" she asked.

"You tell me," he said. "We made a deal. Was last night part of the job?"

She gasped. "Do you think I need to pay someone to make love to me?" Laurel turned on her heel and stalked over to the stove. She dumped a box of pasta into a huge pot, then gave it a stir. "I didn't command you into my shower. I didn't even invite you. You came willingly, as I recall."

"You didn't turn me away." Sean cursed softly. He'd walked in the door fully intending to mend the rift between them. But now it only seemed to be widening. "I don't want to argue."

"What do you want? Tell me."

Sean shook his head. "I can't want anything from this."

"That's not an answer," she said. "Why can't you just say what you feel for once in your life?"

"I don't know what I feel." Sean paced the width of the kitchen. "I care about you. I want to see you happy. But I'm not your husband. And you're not my wife." He took a deep breath. "Since Sinclair is gone, maybe it would be best for me to spend the night at my place."

In truth, he needed to put some distance between them. If he had the time to think, time to put aside thoughts of her beautiful face and incredible body, thoughts that clouded his perceptions, maybe he could figure out what he felt. Feeling anything for a woman was a strange experience and whatever this was that he felt for Laurel was too confusing to sort out in a night.

"No," Laurel said.

"No?"

"I'm paying you to be here and I want you to stay. I've spent most of the afternoon making this dinner and you're required to enjoy it." She grabbed up the bottle of wine and poured a glass, then pushed it at him. "Here, have a drink." A moment later, she retrieved a plate from the refrigerator. "Hors d'oeuvre?"

He plucked a cracker off the tray and popped it into his mouth. "Mmm, very good."

"Are you saying it's good because it is? Or because I'm paying you to say it is?"

"It's good," Sean said.

She seemed pleased and set the plate down on the counter beside him. "I'll just finish dinner. I thought we could eat on the terrace. I've set up the table out there. Why don't you take the wine and salad out and I'll finish cooking the pasta."

He took the salad bowl she offered, tucked the wine in the crook of his arm and walked outside. Considering her mood, dinner promised to be tense. But oddly, her mood didn't bother him as much as he thought it should. She was still the most beautiful, exciting and perplexing woman he'd ever met.

The table was set with crystal and silver and gleaming china. Sean noticed the candles in the center and picked up a book of matches to light them. The setting looked decidedly romantic, the table placed near the edge of the terrace overlooking the gardens and pool.

The candles flickered in the night, a gentle breeze

stirring up the air. He poured a glass of wine for himself and wandered over to the low wall that surrounded the terrace. There were so many things he wanted to say to Laurel, but he wasn't sure how to say them. Words didn't come easily to him; less so, expressions of emotion. But he did feel something for her and it ran deep.

Sean glanced up and saw her struggling with a tray as she stepped through the door. He jogged over to her and took the tray, then offered a smile to soothe her temper. "It smells good," he murmured.

They sat and Laurel pulled the covers off the plates. Sean was impressed with the meal, but politely waited for her to take the first bite. She picked up her fork but before she could, he impulsively raised his wineglass. "Maybe we should have a toast," he murmured.

"To what?" she asked.

"How about to friendship?"

She hesitated, then raised her glass and touched it to his. "All right. To friendship." A tentative smile touched her lips and she took a sip.

Their dinner began in silence, but as they started on the main course, Laurel ventured a comment. "Alistair helped me with the meal. He knows about us, that we're not really married."

"I know he knows," Sean said, wondering if she'd be angry.

"You didn't tell me?"

"You had a lot on your mind."

She nodded. "Alistair said you went to see your family today."

"I talked to my mother—for the first time in my life that I can remember."

"I thought your mother left the family when you were young," she said.

Sean was surprised she remembered the conversation they'd had. "She did. She came back to Boston a year ago last January with my sister, Keely, who was born after my mother left. I haven't been able to talk to her since she returned."

"Why not?"

He'd kept the feelings bottled up inside for so long that he wasn't sure he could express them in words. But as he looked at Laurel, he knew she'd be the one to understand. "I don't know. I was angry at her. I didn't trust her. When I was little, I used to believe she was my angel, watching over me from heaven. My father had told us she'd died in a car wreck."

"And she hadn't?" Laurel said, her expression filled with sympathy. "That must have been very confusing for you."

He picked up his wineglass and took a gulp of the wine. "I went to fetch my da from the pub one night," he began, measuring each word. "And he was boasting to his buddies that he'd sent my ma packing because she'd been with another man. That's when I started to hate her. I blamed her for all the bad things that happened to us. But I never told anyone about what I'd heard."

"That's a pretty big secret for a kid to carry around."

"It was like weight that dragged me down. I didn't let myself feel anything. And today I found out that I was wrong. She didn't break her marriage vows. I'm not sure what to do with that revelation."

"Let it go," Laurel said. "After my mother died, I carried around an anger for her that I couldn't understand. I was ten and she'd left me and I blamed her because she didn't fight harder. If she loved me, she could have beaten the cancer." She paused, as if her emotions were about to overflow. "And then, one day, I just let it go. And memories of the good times came back and I could love her again."

"I don't have any memories," Sean said.

"Then make some new ones," Laurel urged. "Spend some time with your mother, take her out to lunch, find out who she is. At least you have that chance. Don't waste it."

Sean reached across the table and slipped his hand around her nape, gently pulling her toward him. The kiss began as simple gratitude, but then, after a few moments, it became more—an apology, a promise, an invitation. They both stumbled to their feet, the table still between them.

He stepped around it, his mouth locked on hers, then pulled Laurel into his arms. All the anger had faded, replaced by need, stronger than anything he'd felt the night before. He wanted to make love to her right then, to reassure himself that she truly did care for him. He needed Laurel more than he'd ever needed a woman in his life.

Sean cupped her face in his hands and stared down into her eyes. "How did you get so smart?" He kissed her again, letting his hands drift over her body, taking in the soft curves and sweet angles as if they belonged solely to him.

He was tempted to drag her up to bed, to show her how much he needed her. But last night's encounter had left them both anxious and confused, ripe for the argument they'd had. They needed time to sort out these feelings, time to let them grow naturally. He groaned inwardly. Every instinct told him to enjoy her while he could. But Sean wasn't interested in short-term pleasure. If there was something real between him and Laurel, he needed to know, and this was the only way to find out.

Sean gently set her back from him and smiled. "Dinner is getting cold."

She swallowed hard and forced a smile. "Right. Dinner."

They passed the rest of the evening in easy conversation, Sean surprised at how good it felt to discuss his childhood with her. She listened and offered her thoughts, then questioned him, prompting him to reveal more. But through it all, the kiss they'd shared hung between them like a ticking alarm clock just waiting to go off. With every minute that passed, Sean wondered how much longer he could resist touching her.

He managed to make it through dessert and then helped her clear the table and do the dishes. As they worked, they finished the bottle of wine, both of them relaxing into each other. And when the dishes were finished and the kitchen cleaned, the next step was obvious.

It would be so easy to walk up the stairs with her

and to make love to her for the rest of the night. But for the first time since he'd met her, he believed that there was something special between them, something that needed to be treated with greater care—something that just might last.

Laurel wiped her hands on a kitchen towel, then carefully folded it and set it aside. "It's late," she said, glancing up at the clock. "Nearly midnight."

Sean slipped his arms around her waist and pulled her near. His lips found hers again and he kissed her, gently exploring her mouth. When he stepped back, her eyes were still closed. "Time for bed."

Laurel opened her eyes and he caught a flicker of apprehension there. "Right. I am tired. And you've had a busy day."

"And since Sinclair isn't here, I think it would be better if I found another place to sleep."

A look of surprise suffused her pretty features. She opened her mouth, as if ready to protest, then suddenly snapped it shut. "You don't want to sleep with me?"

"Of course I do," Sean said. "But I think we need to be a little more careful, don't you?"

"Careful?" She paused as if trying to come to grips with his reasoning. "You're right." Laurel cleared her throat. "So, I guess I'll see you in the morning."

"Thanks for dinner," Sean said, smoothing his hand over her cheek. "It was very nice." He kissed her once more, doing his best to keep his desires in check. And then she walked out, his gaze following her until the kitchen door swung shut.

Sean inhaled a deep breath and let it out slowly. He

waited a few minutes, then followed her up the stairs. As he passed her bedroom door, Sean stopped, fighting the temptation to go inside and to lose himself in her incredible body. He imagined her slipping out of the sexy black dress she'd worn, then discarding the lacy scraps of underwear. He imagined himself running his hands over her naked body and gently laying her down on the bed.

A soft moan slipped from his lips and he turned from the door. If he planned to get any sleep at all, he'd have to find a room as far away from Laurel's as possible. "It's going to be a long night," he murmured.

But he couldn't wait for tomorrow. The way he felt now, anything was possible.

7

LAUREL RAKED HER HAIR out of her eyes and slowly descended the stairs, following the scent of coffee. Since Alistair was still in New York with Sinclair, Sean must have risen early—at least, earlier than 10:00 a.m., which was when she'd finally rolled out of bed.

She'd spent a restless night, unable to sleep or to stop thinking about Sean. Somewhere in the house, he'd fallen into a bed and she wondered if he'd slept at all or if he, too, had been plagued with memories of the night they'd spent together. It seemed so silly to sleep alone when they'd shared so much passion just twenty-four hours before.

After their dinner conversation, she felt closer than ever to Sean. They'd tipped the balance of their relationship and she didn't want to set it right again. This was now as much about pleasure as it was about business.

Did he really care for her or was this still just about a paycheck? What would he do if she suddenly decided not to pay him? She'd promised him twenty thousand at the end of their month together, but what if she informed him that she didn't plan to pay? That it, in fact, didn't feel right to pay? Would he still want to stay? Did his feelings for her run deep enough to survive the end of their "marriage"?

Laurel sighed, then stopped to study her reflection in a tall mirror. What had begun as such a simple plan had turned her life upside down. And the man she'd hired to be her husband had become something so much more. Falling in love with Sean Quinn hadn't been part of the plan.

Satisfied that she looked as good as she could in her sleep-deprived state, Laurel pushed open the swinging door of the kitchen. She froze when she saw a pretty woman standing next to Sean, sipping a cup of coffee and chatting with him. She was dressed in a flattering summer dress that hugged her slender figure.

They both turned to look at her and Sean smiled. "Good morning," he said. He crossed the room and took Laurel's arm, pulling her toward the stranger. His touch should have sent her pulse racing, but she felt as if her heart had ground to a stop.

"Hi," Laurel said, glancing back and forth between the two of them.

The woman stepped forward and held out her hand. "Hi. I'm Amy Quinn. I'm Sean's sister-in-law. You must be Laurel."

The tiny stab of jealousy she'd felt a moment ago slowly faded as she shook Amy's hand. "Hello." She glanced over at Sean. "Have you come to visit Sean?"

"She's come to see you," he said. "I asked Amy to stop by."

His response caught her off guard. Why would Sean ask a member of his family to visit her? Though she'd met Seamus, Sean hadn't seemed anxious to introduce her to any other Quinns.

"I came to talk to you about your plan," Amy explained.

Stunned, Laurel sent Sean an accusing glare. "You told her about our plan? Did you tell her about Eddie? About how he—"

"Who's Eddie?" Amy asked.

"That's another plan." Sean turned back to Laurel. "I didn't tell her about that plan. I told her about your plan. For the children's center. I thought she might want to hear about it. Amy runs a charitable foundation. She gives people money for good causes."

"I don't give money away—the foundation board does," Amy corrected.

Laurel glanced back and forth between them. "But I don't—"

"Just tell her what you want to do," Sean insisted. He stepped over to the counter and poured a cup of coffee, then handed it to Laurel. "I put some doughnuts on the table outside. Why don't you go out there and talk?"

Given that she really had no choice in the matter, Laurel nodded. Amy Quinn seemed like a nice enough person. And if Sean thought his sister-in-law had something to offer, then the least Laurel could do was listen.

"So, I understand you and Sean got married last weekend," Amy said as they strolled out to the terrace.

Laurel stumbled slightly. "He told you about that?"

"No. I got that through the Quinn family grapevine. It's becoming a very effective way to get news."

"We aren't really married," Laurel said. "It was just for show. It's a long story."

"That's too bad. About the marriage, I mean. He seems to care about you very much. I've never seen him so...smitten."

They sat and Laurel set her coffee in front of her. "He's a very special man."

Amy picked up a doughnut and laughed. "Good grief, if they aren't eating a heaping plate of cholesterol for breakfast, the Quinn boys are scarfing down pounds of refined sugar." She set the doughnut back on the plate and smiled at Laurel. "He is a very special man. And he deserves a special woman."

Her meaning couldn't have been any clearer. How wonderful it must be for Sean to have a family that looked out for him. She'd never really known that feeling, being an only child and losing her parents so early in her life. She envied Amy's place among the Quinns.

"Sean told me he has five brothers, but I don't know much about them. He doesn't say much."

"Tall, dark, handsome and very silent," Amy teased. "I have to say, our conversation before you joined us amounted to the most I'd ever heard him say. I don't know what you've done to him, but it's had a good effect."

"So his family is close?"

"Very close. All the brothers and Keely live in Boston. They're all married or engaged to be married. I'm married to Brendan, the third brother. Sean is the..." She frowned. "I can never remember if he's fourth or fifth. I think Brian popped out first."

"Popped out?"

She took a sip of her coffee, then reached inside her purse to retrieve a small pad of paper. "Sean has a twin brother, Brian. He's a reporter for the *Globe*. He used to be on WBTN. They're twins. Some people can't tell the difference, but I don't think they look anything alike."

Laurel swallowed a gasp. Sean had never told her he had a twin. Wasn't that the kind of news a guy shared with the woman he— She stopped short. He didn't love her. She was just the woman he'd slept with and there were no rules when it came to casual sex. In fact, the less information exchanged, the better.

"So, let's get down to business," Amy suggested. "I run the Aldrich-Sloane Family Foundation."

Laurel gasped, the name causing a sudden burst of memory. "You're Amy Aldrich Sloane! You were two years ahead of me at Sandborne Country Day. You probably don't remember me, but I remember you. You used to wear all that black leather with your school uniform. And you had that pink streak in your hair. I used to think you were so wild."

"I remember you," Amy said, her expression brightening. "Laurie Rand. My goodness, I didn't make the connection."

Laurel hadn't had many friends at school. After her mother had died, she'd withdrawn, unable to feel comfortable with friends who had whole and complete families. Amy probably remembered a lot more that went unsaid—Laurel Rand was the girl who sat alone at lunch, the girl who preferred the solitude of the library to the chatter of the quad, the girl who seemed to be lost among the crowd. Though she and Amy shared the same background, both of them from wealthy families, the Aldrich-Sloane fortune had been far more vast than the Rand fortune, a fact that put Amy way above Laurel in the pecking order at Sandborne Country Day.

Laurel had enough money to do one good thing, but Amy's family could do so much more. "I have a trust fund," Laurel began. "I was supposed to get it when I was twenty-six."

"Me, too," Amy said, nodding. "I never understood why twenty-six was such a magic number. Although I'm glad I had to wait. If I had gotten that money any earlier, I would have blown it all."

"I'm also required to be married. If I'm not, then I have to wait until I'm thirty-one, which will be too late."

"Too late?"

"I have a…a project. I want to start an after-school community center in Dorchester, near where I used to teach school." As she spoke about her project to a complete stranger, the dream of it began to become more of a reality. In her mind she could see the place as it might look two or three years from now, filled with children looking for that one thing that made them feel special, that one talent that they possessed that set them apart.

There had been so many times after her mother died, when she'd felt lost and alone, when just simple encouragement might have brightened an otherwise gloomy day. She wanted to give that to others. She wanted to give them wings.

"The center would specialize in the arts, offering free dance and music lessons, and drama and painting classes. And we'd have a space so that groups could come in and perform for the children, and a gallery where we could display some of the kids' work. I already have a building in Dorchester in mind, an old storefront, and I think it would be perfect. It's right on the bus line and—"

"How much do you have?" Amy asked.

"I don't have anything right now. But I should have five million soon."

"If that becomes the basis for your endowment, you can expect to bring in about three-hundred thousand a year in interest and that's if you invest wisely and the economy is good. That's almost enough to pay the bills and provide a salary for yourself and a staff. Five million sounds like a lot, but it really isn't."

Laurel's heart fell and tears pressed at the corners of her eyes. If Amy Quinn didn't think the project was possible, then maybe Laurel's dreams would never become reality. "You don't think I can make this work. But I know I can. I've been in the schools and there's so little time devoted to the arts. I want to give these kids more. And I—"

"I think it's a wonderful idea," Amy interrupted. "I'm just saying that I think you should try to get funding beyond what you have in your own trust fund. If you don't use your own money, it's going to be tougher, but it could still be done. Then your trust fund could be used for emergencies or as an endowment." She paused. "You still need to have money to renovate. We may be able to fund that. You'd need to put together a plan, a budget and an outline of your curriculum. But I think there's a good chance we can give you enough to get the place up and running. Of course, we'll need to see how you plan to keep the place running and where the money will come from. I can suggest some people who could help you apply for grants. There are a lot of other foundations that would probably give to such a great cause."

Laurel sat back in her chair. "I can't believe it," she said. "It can't be this easy."

"Oh, it will never be easy," Amy said. "But you seem to be passionate about this cause, and that's the most important thing." Amy glanced over her shoulder and Laurel followed her gaze, noticing Sean just inside the doorway, pacing back and forth. Amy waved at him, then handed Laurel a business card. "Call me and we'll set up an appointment. I'll help you with your proposal. And if the board approves it, you'll be on your way." She stood, but instead of shaking Laurel's hand, she gave her a quick hug. "I hope everything turns out for you, Laurel. Not just for your project, but with Sean. It would be nice if the Mighty Quinn curse finally claimed its last victim."

"The Mighty Quinn curse? What's that?"

Amy laughed. "It's a very long story. Maybe you can convince Sean to tell you about it sometime."

She walked to the door and gave Sean a kiss on the cheek as she passed. "I'll see myself out," Amy said. "And don't be such a stranger. Bring Laurel over to the pub sometime. Everyone is anxious to meet her."

Sean stepped out of the house and slowly crossed the terrace to where Laurel stood. A flood of emotion raced through her and she didn't know what to say. In one simple move, Sean had made her dream come true. With hard work and determination, she could make the center happen without her trust fund and without Sinclair's approval.

"Thank you," she said, not sure whether to laugh or to cry. "Thank you so much."

"It went well? She liked your idea?"

Laurel threw her arms around Sean's neck and hugged him hard. "Yes! She said it was a good idea. And if her board of directors agrees, her foundation will give me money to get the center started. All I have to do is—"

Her words were stopped by his kiss. Sean cupped her face in his hands as his mouth covered hers. A tiny moan slipped from her throat. It seemed as if weeks had passed since he'd last kissed her. In reality, it was barely twelve hours.

When he finished with her lips, he moved to her eyes and her nose. "I missed you," he murmured.

"I missed you, too."

"I didn't sleep last night. I couldn't."

"I couldn't, either," Laurel said. "Maybe we should go back to bed."

He hesitated for just a moment and Laurel thought he might find some excuse to refuse her invitation. But then he bent and swung her into his arms, carrying her through the house and up the stairs. Laurel wanted to thank him for all he'd done. And she couldn't think of a better way.

SHE WAS THE MOST beautiful woman he'd ever touched, ever kissed. And Laurel was the only woman he'd ever loved. Sean moved above her, knowing his release was just a heartbeat away. This had to be love. He'd never felt anything as powerful as what he felt for Laurel when he was deep inside of her.

He rolled to the side and pulled her on top of him, her legs straddling his hips. But the sight of her naked body, her hair curled around her face, her skin gleaming in the low light, was more than he could handle. He grabbed her hips and stopped her from moving, holding his breath as he fought his release.

"Don't," he murmured. "Don't move."

Laurel opened her eyes, smiled at him, then brushed a kiss across his lips. "I won't move." A current of pleasure shot through him as she shifted above him, but he refused to give in.

He took her face in his hands, furrowing his fingers through her hair. Laurel arched back, closing her eyes as she braced her hands on his chest. He wanted to tell her how he felt, but he was afraid if he said it out loud and she didn't return his sentiments, he might never be able to say the words again. This feeling he had when they were together, this undeniable need to possess her and to move inside her, to lose himself in her body, would never go away—even if she did.

Sean reached between them and touched her, bringing her closer to the edge. Laurel moaned, then moved against his hand. And then, suddenly, she sucked in a sharp breath and shuddered. Sean felt her body spasm around him and, without moving, he let himself come.

His orgasm was quiet yet powerful and he watched her cry out in pleasure, his shaft still buried to the hilt. His heart slammed in his chest and he gasped when she finally moved, taking the last he had to offer. With a low moan, Laurel collapsed on top of him, nuzzling her face into his neck.

"We can take a nap, if you like," she murmured.

He stroked her back from her nape to the delicious curve of her backside, enjoying the feel of her skin beneath his palms. "I'm not sleepy anymore."

Laurel pushed up next to him, her hair tickling his chest. "Amy said something to me earlier. She said you'd been cursed. A family curse. What did she mean?"

"It's stupid," he said.

"Tell me," Laurel insisted.

He'd opened his heart to her already, each time surprised at how easy it was. At first, he'd thought it was just Laurel and the trust he felt when he was with her. But maybe it more about the "marriage" they shared. He'd had a chance to experience what marriage might be. He'd allowed himself to believe that she might be there for him, not just for a day or a month, but for the rest of his life.

All the benefits of marriage, but without the commitment, he mused. Suddenly, avoiding the Quinn curse didn't seem so important. "My father used to tell us stories when we were younger about our Mighty Quinn ancestors. Our ancestors were always strong and clever and heroic. A lot of the stories he told were old Irish fables and myths, but he always gave them a twist. The women characters were always the enemy."

"Why was that?"

Sean shrugged. "My da was a man scorned by a woman and he wanted to protect us from the same fate. The stories had the desired effect. Seamus Quinn's six sons were bachelors, until the family curse hit a few years ago."

"What is the curse?"

"I'm not sure if there really is one. My da thinks it goes way back in Ireland—he's got some story that explains it all. Here in Boston, it started with Conor. He met his wife, Olivia, when he rescued her from a local mobster. And Dylan rescued Meggie from a fire, and Brendan saved Amy from a bar brawl."

"I don't understand how that can be a curse," Laurel said. "A curse is a bad thing and they did good things."

"The curse is that they fell in love with the women they rescued," Sean explained. "In Seamus's eyes, my brothers were victims, not heroes. And I'm the last one left."

Laurel ran her fingers over his forehead, pushing his hair out of his eyes. "If you don't want to be a victim, then don't rescue anyone."

"I already did," Sean said.

"Who?"

"You. I saved you from Edward."

A long silence grew between them as the implications of his words sank in. Maybe he didn't have to tell her that he loved her. Maybe she'd understand on her own. If he believed in the curse, then it wasn't a choice for him—he was destined to love her.

"Tell me one of those stories," she said.

Sean groaned. "I'm not good with the stories. Brendan is the best. And Brian tells a pretty good tale. I'll just mess it up."

"Try," she said. She bit his neck playfully. "If you tell me a story, I'll give you ten kisses."

"Ten? I'll settle for twenty."

"Fifteen," she said. "Fifteen very long, deep, wet

kisses for one story. It's a fair price. You're not going to get a better deal anywhere else."

Sean didn't have any intention of shopping around. He liked the way Laurel kissed. "I'll tell you a story about a merrow named Duana. A merrow is like a mermaid. Very beautiful. Mermen aren't seen often, but in ancient Ireland, the merrows often took mortals as their lovers. There are some Irish families who actually believe they descend from the merrows." He paused. "I want a down payment."

Laurel giggled and then kissed him, putting everything she had into it, seducing him with her lips and her tongue, pressing her naked body against his. "Go on," she said when she finished.

"Duana, like the other merrows, dressed in a cloak made of sealskin, and when she wrapped herself in her cloak, she could swim in the deepest, coldest water, just like a seal. But to walk on land, she had to leave her cloak at the edge of the water. This was dangerous. If a mortal found a merrow's cloak, then he had power over her and she couldn't return to the sea. This is what happened with Duana. One day, Kelan Quinn, a poor fisherman, found her cloak and took it, thinking that it might keep him warm in the damp winters of Ireland. He knew that it was a valuable cloak and so he hid it well in the thatched roof of his cottage for safekeeping until winter came."

"If a merrow doesn't go back to the sea, will she die?"

Sean frowned. "I don't think so. Conor would probably know. I think they just long for the sea because it's their home. Many farmers and fishermen wanted to trap a merrow because merrows are very rich. They have chests of gold and silver and jewels that they've taken from shipwrecks. But Kelan didn't know that he'd taken the cloak of a merrow. And when a beautiful woman appeared at his door the next day, he let her inside.

"Merrows are part of the fairy world and so they don't really care about mortals, except to use them as lovers now and then. But mortals can fall in love with merrows and this happened to Kelan. Duana was so beautiful that he wanted her for his wife. But Duana told him that she couldn't marry him until he gave her a gift. Kelan was a poor fisherman and could think of nothing that Duana might appreciate. He had a few pence in his pocket, but that was all. He was desperate to find something to convince Duana of his love. And then he thought of the sealskin cloak. He retrieved it from his roof and Duana slipped it on. With a laugh, she ran down to the sea and jumped in, disappearing beneath the waves."

"What happened to Kelan?" Laurel asked.

"He was devastated. He thought he'd fallen in love with a madwoman, so he dove into the sea and began to search for her, hoping to save Duana from drowning. But the sea was cold and he couldn't stay in the water long. Again and again, he went back to shore and as soon as he could, he swam back out to the sea. Exhausted, he dove one last time and as the water overwhelmed him he came face to face with Duana, her long hair swirling around her head. She took his hand and pulled him deeper and deeper. And only then did Kelan realize who and what she really was.

He tore her cloak from her body and swam hard for the surface, wrapping himself in the sealskin."

"What happened to Duana?"

"She died. And Kelan, clever Quinn that he was, used her cloak to swim in the sea and retrieved the treasure Duana had collected. The poor fisherman became the richest man in his village because he'd outsmarted a merrow."

Sean didn't realize until he'd finished the story how many parallels there were between him and Laurel and the poor fisherman and his beautiful merrow. Like the merrow, Laurel had seduced him, and though she was wealthy, the treasure of her body was what Sean really coveted. Would she pull him under like Duana had? And if she did, would he be able to escape?

"The end," Sean added. "I told you I wasn't good with the stories."

"No," Laurel said. "You told it very well. It just doesn't have a very happy ending. And it's not very romantic."

"But to my father, the story taught a valuable lesson."

"Don't steal coats from the beach?" Laurel asked.

Sean chuckled. "No. Beware of beautiful women."

"And what about me?" Laurel asked. "Are you supposed to beware of me?"

Grabbing her waist, he rolled her over and pinned her beneath him. Staring down at her exquisite features, Sean still couldn't believe the luck that had brought him into her life. "You? I have to be very careful around you. I think you could break my heart if you wanted to."

Laurel reached up and ran her hand over his cheek. "Why would I break your heart?" Her hand moved to his chest. "Your heart is what I love most about you."

Sean's breath stilled in his throat as the impact of her words hit him full force. Had she just said she loved him? He should have felt a wild sense of exhilaration, and he did, for one brief moment. But then, an uneasy fear set in. He wanted to believe her words, but she'd said them so casually, tossed them out there as if they really didn't mean a thing.

He kissed her, losing himself in the sweet taste of her mouth, hoping to soothe his doubts with the pleasures her body offered. Would he be like Kelan Quinn, lured into love and then tricked out of it? Or could he chart his own course, putting all those stories about his Quinn ancestors behind him?

For now, he'd keep his feelings locked safely away. And someday, maybe, he'd be brave...or clever...or strong enough to hand Laurel the key.

"I THINK you'll need to replace all these windows."

Laurel stood beside Sean, a clipboard clutched in her hand. "How much do you think windows cost? Maybe we should just try to replace the broken glass. That would be cheaper, wouldn't it?"

Sean slipped his arm around her waist and pulled her close. They'd come to Dorchester to evaluate the building, but it was clear that neither of them had a clue as to what needed to be done to make it habitable. In truth, he'd have rather stayed at home, in bed with Laurel, the way they had for the past three days.

It had been a honeymoon of sorts that began after Alistair called to say that he and Sinclair would be staying in New York for a few extra days. Night had turned into day and then back to night again and they'd been unaware of the world outside the house. They'd slept when they were tired and made love beside the pool in the middle of the night. Food varied from pizza to Chinese, whatever could be delivered. Sean had always thought of a honeymoon as a silly excuse to take a trip. But now he knew just what purpose it served. He felt as if he and Laurel had become one person, two sides of the same coin, completely in sync with each other's bodies and thoughts, needs and desires.

He glanced down at her, noticing the tiny lines of stress around her mouth. The urge to wipe them away with a kiss was strong, but he decided against it. "We'll need screens so we can open the windows," she murmured, scribbling on her pad.

"I think you're going to want to air-condition this place," Sean said. "You'll have to run duct work since this is all radiant heat. But you've got high ceilings and they can leave it exposed."

"What's radiant heat?" Laurel asked.

"Those radiators over there have hot water in them and they radiate heat instead of forced air which—" Sean sighed. "We're not going to be able to do this. Give me your cell phone." As she rummaged through her purse, Sean grabbed his wallet and found the business card he'd saved. He took the phone from Laurel and punched in a number.

"Who are you calling? Do you know an air-conditioning guy?"

The receptionist at Kencor answered after one ring.

"Rafe Kendrick, please. Tell him it's his brother-in-law, Sean Quinn."

A few moments later Rafe came on the line. "Sean. Hi. What's up? Is everything all right?"

The surprise of hearing from Sean was apparent in Rafe's voice. Sean wasn't sure he'd ever carried on a conversation with his brother-in-law. He had held Rafe's arms to help out when the other Quinn men had been all set to pummel him, but that had been the extent of their contact. Rafe hadn't exactly been welcomed into the Quinn family, though the brothers had called a truce since he and Keely had married. "I need a favor," Sean said.

"Anything. What can I do for you?"

"I have a friend who wants to renovate a building in Dorchester. It's in pretty rough shape and she needs to get an estimate of the costs."

"Does she have an architectural plan?" Rafe asked.

"No, I don't think so."

"Well, she'll need that first."

"She doesn't have a lot of money for this project," Sean said. "She wants to turn the building into a community center for children."

"Ah, this is the woman Amy met. Keely talked to Amy and she mentioned that you had a..." His voice faded. "Well, why don't I send over one of my architects? We'll get him started with some rough sketches."

"How much is this going to cost?" Sean asked.

"Don't worry about that. This is family. Give me the address and I'll send someone over. Are you there now?"

"Yeah." Sean gave Rafe the address.

"I'll have someone there in thirty minutes. Once your friend has a plan, I'll have someone on my staff work up some estimates. I've got a lot of contractors who owe me favors. I could use my—"

"No," Sean said. "You've done enough. Thanks. I appreciate it."

"No problem," he said.

Sean turned off the phone and handed it back to Laurel. "We're all set," he said. "Rafe is sending an architect over to talk to you about your plans."

"I can't afford to pay an—"

"Don't worry. He's doing a favor. I'm family."

Laurel shook her head. "Family," she repeated. "It's like the Quinns are a corporation. Is there anything you can't get done?"

"Probably not. Amy can fund the place, Rafe can fix it up. Brian can probably write a story for the *Globe* and Liam can take promotional photos. Olivia could track down some used furniture and Lily could get you some good PR. And Eleanor is a banker, so she could keep track of the money."

"And what will you do for me?"

Sean grinned and dropped a kiss on her lips. "I provide relaxation and moral support."

Laurel hugged him, then pulled away and wandered over to an old sink that hung from the wall. "What are you going to use your money for?"

"What money?" Sean asked.

She slowly turned. "The money I'm paying you. What are you going to do with it?"

Sean had forgotten all about the money. That's what

had drawn him to her in the first place, but now it seemed insignificant. "I was thinking about getting an office. I've been putting some cash away lately. It's hard to get corporate clients when I'm working out of my apartment. I need a place to do business."

"Is private investigations pretty lucrative?"

"For some guys." Not for Bert Hinshaw, Sean mused. The old P.I. had never even made enough to buy himself a decent suit. And now that he was getting on in years, he had nothing to show for his life, except a beat-up Cadillac convertible and a drinking habit that drained his wallet as quickly as he could fill it. Sean didn't want to end up like Bert. He wanted a life he could be proud of, a life that meant something.

"What about you?" Laurel asked.

Her reasons for asking were clear. A rich girl like Laurel Rand couldn't marry an ordinary guy like Sean Quinn. Hell, he usually had to scrape together spare change to pay the rent. He drove a beat-up car and didn't even own a decent suit. And she had five million burning a hole in her pocket. "I'm never going to be a millionaire like you," he said.

"Is that important to you?"

"No. Is it important to you?"

Laurel shook her head. "Don't get me wrong. It's nice to have money. But I'd give every last dollar back to have a family. To have a mother and father. And sisters and brothers. People who care about me. It sounds trite, but money can't buy everything. It can't buy love."

"It bought you a husband," Sean said.

She smiled weakly. "But only for a month. After the

month is up, you're going to go home. Maybe even sooner if Amy approves my plan." She wandered across the room and began to measure the windows on the far wall.

Suddenly, Sean regretted his call to Rafe. If Amy funded Laurel's project, then Laurel would have no use for his services. She'd write him a check and send him packing. A knot tightened in his gut when he thought about leaving Laurel. He wasn't ready to let her go, wasn't ready to be dismissed from her life. Yet he wasn't ready to ask her to marry him, either.

There was an easy way to know how she really felt, he mused. He could simply throw all his cards on the table and admit he was madly in love with her. Sean knew he'd be able to see her response in her eyes. Over the past week he'd learned to read her feelings pretty well.

If he knew how she felt, if he could somehow be assured that her feelings would last, then maybe he could take the chance. But he had to be careful not to expect too much. Even if Laurel did love him, what guarantees did he have that she'd feel the same way in a month or a year or ten years? Fiona Quinn had loved her husband and her family and she'd walked away when times got tough. Laurel could do the same.

Sean combed his fingers through his hair. Why had things been so easy for his brothers and so complicated for himself? They'd all fallen in love and known exactly what they wanted in a matter of weeks.

Maybe this wasn't the Quinn family curse at all. And maybe Laurel wasn't the woman he was destined to love for the rest of his life. Or maybe he just needed a little more time.

8

LAUREL SMOOTHED THE SKIRT of her loose cotton dress and checked the row of tiny buttons that decorated the front. "How do I look?" she asked.

"You look absolutely beautiful." Sean grimaced as he slipped the knot of his tie up to his collar. "Are you sure I have to wear a tie?"

She stepped up to him and readjusted the knot. "It's only for a little while. We'll have drinks and then dinner with Sinclair and then you can take off the tie. You know, you're going to have to start wearing a tie for business. It makes you look more respectable and a P.I. should look trustworthy."

"I can get one of those clip-on ties," Sean muttered, gently pushing her hands away. He turned to the mirror and tugged at the knot.

Laurel ran her hands over his shoulders. "I think Sinclair wants to talk to us about my trust fund. Alistair hinted that they'd discussed it while they were in New York." Her gaze met Sean's in the reflection of the mirror and his fingers stilled.

"So then this will be over?" he asked.

She nodded. "I'll write you a big fat check and you can go home—as soon as Sinclair leaves and the check clears the bank."

"Is that what you want?"

Laurel smiled, trying to appear nonchalant. No, it wasn't what she wanted, but Sean wasn't offering anything more. She'd given him every opportunity to reveal the depth of his feelings. Yet when it came to serious discussion about their future, he'd turned into a brick wall. In the beginning, she'd found his silence intriguing, but now it was a source of frustration. "That was the deal."

"Right," Sean said.

Taking a deep breath, Laurel walked to the door. "Let's go."

It had been almost impossible to keep her growing feelings for Sean in check. She'd caught herself time and time again with the words on the tip of her tongue. She wanted to tell him she loved him, wanted to shout it until he believed it. But for the first time in her life, she'd restrained her impulsiveness, keeping her mouth shut and her feelings to herself. Maybe a little bit of Sean's nature had rubbed off on her.

They walked down the stairs together, her hand tucked in his. When they stepped inside the library, Sean gave her fingers an encouraging squeeze. Alistair handed Sean a Guinness and set a glass of white wine for Laurel on the table beside the sofa.

As usual, Sinclair didn't notice their arrival. This time his nose was buried in the latest copy of *Stamp Aficionado* magazine. But Laurel wasn't about to play his game. She'd go on the offensive, the way Sean had the first time he and Sinclair had met. "How was the auction, Uncle? Did you get the coin you wanted?"

Sinclair peered over the top of his magazine. "You look different," he said.

"Thank you," Laurel replied, wondering if it was because of the new shade of lipstick she wore or the flush of sexual satisfaction on her cheeks.

"I didn't say you looked good, I said you looked different."

"Well, I'm glad to see you noticed something about me. That's a positive step."

Sinclair dropped his magazine. "Your dress has roses on it."

"No, these are peonies, not roses. There's a difference."

"How did the auction go?" Sean asked, sitting next to Laurel and putting an end to the verbal sparring.

Sinclair pointed to a wooden box on the coffee table in front of him. "She's a beauty," he said. "Take a look."

Sean opened the box and examined the coin. "You know what I find so amazing about your coins?"

"What is that, Edward?"

"That the thing you love the most, you can hold in your hand." He picked up the coin. "You can close your fist around it and never let it go. No one can take it from you, either. There aren't many things in life that are so safe."

Laurel held her breath, startled by Sean's words. Was he talking about the coin, or was he talking about her? Sinclair had done his best to chain her to this house and to his silly rules about her inheritance. She felt like one of his coins, a possession he really didn't need, but couldn't let anyone else have, a possession that he held so tightly he nearly destroyed it in the process.

Sean opened his fist and handed the coin back to Sinclair. "She is beautiful," he said.

"Yes, she is," Sinclair replied. He glanced at Laurel, his gaze meeting hers for the first time in years. "I suppose we had better talk about your trust fund." He moved his gaze back to Sean. "You are aware that Laurel is an heiress. Her father left her a sizable trust that he gave me the responsibility of administrating. I decided Laurel should get the money after her twenty-sixth birthday and after she married."

"She's told me," Sean said.

"I've structured the trust so that Laurel's husband will have no claim to the money."

Sean shrugged. "That doesn't concern me. I didn't marry Laurel for her money."

Laurel suddenly realized that she wasn't breathing. She gulped in a quick breath and tried to calm her nerves. She'd come into the room expecting to be handed a check. She hadn't counted on an inquisition.

"Why did you marry Laurel?" Sinclair asked.

"Because I love her."

"And you expect your marriage to last?"

Sean nodded. "Yes."

"All right." Sinclair held up his hand and Alistair placed a check in it. Laurel tried to contain her excitement. Her dream was so close, she could almost feel it. But instead of being overjoyed, she felt a certain measure of dread. Her future was about to begin, and her present—with Sean—would be left behind.

"With all the pressures of modern life," Sinclair intoned, "I feel that I need to make some accommodations for the possibility that this marriage might not be...oh, what is the word I'm searching for...permanent. To that end, I've decided to give you your trust fund over time. You'll get two hundred and fifty thousand today, five hundred thousand on your first wedding anniversary, a million on your second, two million on your third and the balance on your fourth anniversary. If you stay married, you'll have your fortune by the time you're thirty-one. I think this is a reasonable plan."

Laurel stood. "This was not the agreement," she said. "You can't do this. You can't change the rules in the middle of the game."

"I can do whatever I want," Sinclair said, straightening in his chair. "Oh, and one more condition. You and your husband have to continue to live here in the mansion. This is the Rand family home and any Rand family heirs should be brought up here."

"Why would you do this?" Laurel demanded. "Do you want me to hate you?"

"I want you to be happy," Sinclair said, as if the answer were obvious to everyone but her.

"Well, this is a crappy way to prove that." Unable to contain her emotions any longer, Laurel crumpled up the check, threw it at his head and stalked out of the room. Her body trembled uncontrollably and she wasn't sure whether to cry or to scream. She was twenty-six years old and an eighty-year-old man was pulling all the strings! If it continued like this, she'd be an old woman and still be waiting for Sinclair to throw her a few crumbs.

She took the stairs two at a time and ran into her bedroom, slamming the door behind her. Sean's duffel was stuffed under the bed and she found her suitcases on the top shelf of the closet. "I'm through. I've had enough. Uncle Sinclair can just take his millions and shove them up his—" Laurel finished with a curse, then yanked open her dresser and started pulling out clothes at random. "I am out of here." A soft knock sounded on the door. "Go away!" she shouted.

The door opened and Sean stepped inside. He crossed to the bed and stared down at her open suitcase. "What are you doing?"

"I'm finished. I don't care about the money, I don't care about the community center. It was all just a stupid, silly dream. I thought I could do something that my parents would have been proud of, but it's impossible. I'm going to find an apartment and see if the school district will let me substitute teach. I'm going to get on with my life."

Sean held out the crumpled check. "I thought you might want this."

"No. I don't want any of Sinclair's money."

"It's *your* money, Laurel. And this is enough to get started on the renovations. Once Amy comes through, there will be more. You can still make this work. I know you can."

Tears pressed at the corners of her eyes and she fought them back. She wouldn't cry, she couldn't give Sinclair that last little bit of her dignity. But when Sean reached up and cupped her cheek in his palm, one of the tears slipped out.

"I can't do this anymore," she murmured. "I can't fight him any longer." He pulled her into his arms, enveloping her in his embrace. Laurel pressed her face into his chest and sobbed. "I want my life to start and that can't happen here."

"Just give it a little more time," Sean said. "Stay here with me tonight and see how you feel in the morning."

"Why do you care?" she asked.

He tipped her face up until her gaze met his. "I want you to be happy."

"But we can't continue this," she said, throwing up her arms in frustration.

"And why not? Sinclair hasn't asked for any proof that we're married. He'll go back to Maine, we'll live together here at the house when he's around, and go on with our lives when he isn't. Hell, I could live here full-time. It would save on rent."

"You...you'd do that for me?"

"I don't have anything better to do."

"If Sinclair finds out we're not married, he'll hold everything until I'm thirty-one. He might even decide to wait until I'm fifty. That's his choice."

"How is he going to find out? We've fooled him so far."

"If I could afford to pay you for a year, I would. But I can't. At five hundred a day that would be—"

"About a hundred and eighty thousand," Sean said. "And you don't have to pay me."

"You'd stay for no reason?"

"I have my reasons. I want to see you make the community center work. That's reason enough."

"I can't ask you to do that," Laurel said, shaking her head. "You want to get your business off the ground and—"

"I can still do that," Sean said.

She hesitated. "And how would things be?"

"I'd go to work every morning and so would you. We'd come home and have dinner."

"I mean, how would it be between us?" she interrupted. "What would we be to each other?"

Sean considered her question for a long moment. "I don't know. We'd have to figure that out as we went along."

She blinked, then stared down at her hands. She wanted to be his love and his life. She wanted him to promise that he'd stay forever. But he obviously wasn't ready to do that—and maybe he never would be. She'd grown to love the vulnerability in him. But that vulnerability was what kept him from returning her love.

"I—I really appreciate the offer. And I will think about it." Laurel turned and crawled onto the bed, pulling the covers up around her. She felt the bed shift as he lay behind her. He wrapped his arms around her waist, drawing her back against his body.

"We'll figure this out," he reassured her. "We just need to give it a little more time."

A sigh slipped from her throat. Maybe he was right. Laurel was sometimes too impatient for her own good. But how long was she willing to wait for her dream to come true? And how long would it be before Sean Quinn finally admitted that he loved her? Would either come to pass or would she spend her lifetime waiting?

LAUREL STEERED HER CAR into the circular drive of the Rand mansion and pulled it up to the front door. After a restless night's sleep, she'd awakened in Sean's arms, both of them still dressed from the night before. They'd talked quietly and Sean had convinced her to stick to her plan, to leave all her options open for now and not make any rash decisions.

Alistair had prepared a quick breakfast for them both, hovering over them, worried that she was still angry over the argument with her uncle. Laurel wondered why the butler had even bothered to tell her about Sinclair and her mother. If her uncle loved her, then he had a real problem when it came to showing it.

She turned off the ignition and grabbed her purse from the passenger seat, slipping the deposit slip from the bank inside. Sean had been right. A quarter of a million dollars was nothing to sniff at. She could buy a lot of nails and boards and duct work with that kind of money. Once the check cleared the bank, the money was all hers and Sinclair couldn't take it back. Laurel smiled. For once, she'd pulled Sinclair's strings! But she wasn't trying to delude herself. This might be the one and only string she ever got to pull.

If she and Sean made it through a year of their pretend marriage, it would be a major miracle. So many things could go wrong. Sinclair could get suspicious...she might slip up and call Sean by his real name...or— Laurel groaned. Sean might meet another woman and decide he didn't want to be "married" to her anymore.

"This will never work." Every time he left the house, she'd be holding her breath, waiting for the day that he decided not to return. After all, he'd offered to stay out of the goodness of his heart. But what if that heart found another woman to be good to?

Laurel pressed her fingers to her temples and cursed

softly. "One day at a time," she muttered. The next step was to make sure her presentation to the Aldrich-Sloane Family Foundation went well. After that, she'd worry about her marriage—or lack of one.

She stepped out of the car and hurried to the front door. She'd dropped Sean off at his apartment so he could pick up his car and his messages and he'd promised to return before lunch. A nervous knot twisted in her stomach.

Now that she'd decided to carry on with the marriage, it was time to get a few things straight between them. Laurel was not about to spend the next year guessing at his feelings. Either he told her exactly how he felt about her or the deal was off. She'd confront him over chicken salad sandwiches and iced tea.

It was a risk, she mused. But better to know the truth than to spend another minute fantasizing about a man who might never love her. She'd certainly made her feelings crystal clear—or had she? Though she'd never said the words out loud, they'd been implied more than once. And surely her actions revealed what she felt in her heart.

But like Sean, she'd been holding a piece of her heart in reserve. She'd never wanted to fall in love, never wanted to risk losing someone she cared about. Yet that's what love was—one big gamble, one throw of the dice, one chance at the lottery. She sighed. If she didn't get in the game, she'd never win. But if she did, she risked losing it all.

Laurel punched in the code for the front door and reached for the knob. But the door swung open in front of her. She froze, the figure that emerged catching her by complete surprise. "Edward?"

Eddie the Cruiser sent her a charming smile, a smile she'd once found so magnetic but now found too smarmy. "Hello, Laurel." His hand came to rest on her arm and he leaned closer to kiss her cheek, but Laurel danced out of his reach.

"What are you doing here?"

"I came to visit. Aren't you glad to see me?"

"I don't want to see you. After what you did to me, I'm surprised you'd show your face here."

"Oh, but I think you *do* want to see me." He grabbed her arm, his fingers pinching into her flesh, and pulled her away from the door and into the driveway. "After my unfortunate arrest and brief incarceration, I was concerned about you. The minute I got out, I came for a visit. Imagine my surprise when I was greeted by the man who had me arrested. Now, what was his name? I think it was Quinn?"

"Get out of here before I call the police," Laurel warned, yanking her arm from his grasp.

"That got me a little curious, so I went back to the church. The minister told me you got married that day. And he described your groom. Now, I may have made a few mistakes along the way, but at least when I got married, it was for real."

"Don't you dare talk to me about marriage. I trusted you. And you betrayed me."

"And how do you think I feel? You never mentioned the real reason why you wanted to marry me. Or should I say, the five million reasons why. I thought you loved me."

"I never loved you," Laurel said. "Maybe subconsciously I knew all along what a bastard you were and I wouldn't let myself love you."

"But you love this guy who's pretending to be your husband?"

Laurel tilted her chin defiantly. "Maybe I do."

"Or maybe you just want your five million dollars and you're willing to use any sap to get it."

"How do you know about the money?"

Eddie grinned and crossed his arms over his chest, gloating. "Your uncle told me. We had a very nice little talk. I must say, he was surprised to find out the man sleeping in your bed wasn't really Edward Garland Wilson of Palm Beach, Florida, but some lowlife P.I. you picked up on the street."

Without thinking, she balled her fingers into a fist and bent her knees, gathering all the energy and strength she possessed. Then she took a swing at him, punching as hard as she could. But she completely missed his stomach and hit him squarely in the groin. The breath left Eddie's lungs in a big whoosh and he groaned, stumbling backward until he fell to the brick pavement.

Laurel was still standing over him, her fingers clenched, when Sean pulled up behind Eddie's car. He jumped out and ran to her side. "What the hell happened here?"

Laurel rubbed her fist. "I hit him. He's been lying there for about a minute."

"You knocked him down? Did he hit his head?" Sean asked.

"No. He just kind of rolled over and started moaning."

Eddie groaned and rolled over again, still curled up in a ball. A grin slowly curled Sean's lips. "Oh. You hit him *there*."

Laurel stepped up to Eddie. "Maybe I should kick him."

Eddie held up his hand in surrender and Sean grabbed Laurel around the waist and pulled her back. When he'd finally convinced her to stay put, he bent and hauled Eddie to his feet. "I told you to stay away from Laurel." He shoved him toward his car. "Now get the hell out of here before I let her beat the crap out of you."

"That's for me and all the women you scammed," Laurel shouted. "I hope you rot in jail." She picked up a clod of dirt from the flower bed and threw it at Eddie's car as he squealed out of the driveway. As he made the turn onto the street, Laurel sat on the front step and covered her face with her hands.

It was all over. Sinclair knew everything. He'd call the bank and stop payment on her check. He'd probably throw her out on the street for tricking him. And he might even decide she was too irresponsible to handle her money ever.

"Are you all right?" Sean asked.

"Sinclair knows," she said. "Eddie talked to him and he knows everything." Laurel stared up at him and laughed ruefully. "The funny thing is, now that it's over, I don't feel so bad. It makes everything a lot simpler." She pushed to her feet. "I guess I better go face

Sinclair. Or maybe I should just pack my bags and leave before he can say anything."

"I could talk to him for you," Sean offered.

Pushing up on her toes, she kissed his cheek. "I think I've dragged you through my family problems enough for now." She punched in the code for the door. "Stick around. I'll let you know how it goes."

Laurel walked inside and headed straight for the library. If Sinclair wasn't eating in the dining room or sleeping in his bedroom, he'd be in the library pouring over auction catalogs and reference books. It was time to stand up for herself, time to give Sinclair an ultimatum. What did she have to lose?

She didn't bother to knock, instead she just walked in. "All right. I'm not married. There, I said it. I pretended to get married because I wanted my trust fund."

Sinclair looked up from his magazine. He glanced at her hands. "Your fingernails are dirty."

"Did you hear what I said? I'm not married. The man who's been sleeping in my bedroom isn't my husband. He's a man I hired to pretend to be my husband because the man who was supposed to be my husband was already married—to nine different women. And this is all your fault."

"Why is that?" Sinclair asked.

"Because I wanted my trust fund. And I was willing to do anything to get it. So, here's the deal. Either you give me my trust fund right now or you'll never see me again." Laurel crossed her arms beneath her breasts and crossed her fingers for good luck. If Alistair was telling the truth about Sinclair's feelings, maybe Sinclair would simply capitulate.

"You knew my terms," Sinclair said.

"Your terms are ridiculous! That money is my inheritance. My father never meant for you to hold it over my head like some kind of bone I'm supposed to jump for. Are you going to give me my money or not?" she demanded.

"No," Sinclair said.

"Then you'll never see me again." Laurel's heart pounded in her chest. Though she and Sinclair had never been close, he was the only family she had. If she walked away from him, she'd have no one. But when it was clear he wasn't going to give in, Laurel's decision was made. It was over. She turned and walked out of the library.

Alistair was waiting outside, a worried expression on his face. "Miss Laurel, you have to give him time. You can't leave."

Laurel reached out and gave Alistair a hug. "I don't have any choice. I've got to start to living my own life. Thank you for being such a good friend. I do love you, Alistair."

"The feeling is quite mutual," he said.

She forced a smile. "So, I guess I better pack. I'm going to have to find a new apartment. I'm sure Sinclair won't allow me to take any furniture, but I—"

"You take whatever you want," Alistair whispered. He gave her hand a squeeze. "And don't forget that nice man you found. Take him with you, too. I don't think you'll find another as good as him."

Laurel nodded, then headed up the stairs to her bedroom. What was she going to do about Sean? Over the past week he'd become a part of her life, an important part. But it had only been a week, seven days of passion and lust. Would what they'd shared survive outside this house?

She stopped on the stairs and slowly turned. She hadn't realized how hard it would be to leave the only home she'd ever known. There were so many memories of her parents here, so many connections to people she'd lost.

"I'm sorry," she murmured. "I tried to stick it out. It's time for me to move on." Laurel wanted to believe her parents heard her, that their spirits lived in the house, that they would approve. She'd stood up for herself against her tyrant of an uncle and that was the most important thing.

Once again she'd let her emotions color her behavior. That was the way it had always been. She'd careened through her life, making mistake after mistake, searching for her place in the world. But her dream for the children's center was still within her reach. She could make it happen if she really wanted to.

But did the same apply to Sean? Could she make him love her the same way she loved him? Or was a week just not enough time to know how either one of them felt?

SEAN TOSSED A STACK of T-shirts into his duffel bag. In the closet, he found the four brand-new dress shirts that Laurel had purchased for him the day they'd gone shopping. He wasn't sure whether they were his to take, so he decided to leave them behind, along with the two sport jackets, three ties and three pairs of trousers.

His mind flashed back to that first day they'd spent together. They'd had so much fun, first walking through her building in Dorchester and then spending the afternoon shopping like a pair of newlyweds beginning a life together. There were so many good memories that he'd collected in such a short time with Laurel, memories he knew would follow him around for the rest of his life. He'd been given a taste of heaven. Without taking a single vow, he'd had a chance to experience life as a married man, to live day-in and day-out with a beautiful woman, to share her bed—and a passion that he'd never dreamed possible.

Sean had hoped he'd have more time with Laurel, maybe even a month or two. The day he'd walked into the church to tell Laurel her wedding was off, he'd been a different man, cynical about love and marriage, so certain that his life was exactly as he wanted it. And now he was actually able to see the possibilities, to believe that he might have the capacity to find happiness with just one woman.

Boxers, socks and jeans followed his T-shirts into the duffel. It seemed as if he had just unpacked yesterday. Sean sighed. He loved her, that much was true. But his feelings were so new and untested he couldn't trust them. Life with Laurel had been a fantasy. But he wouldn't know if his feelings were real or imagined until they were tested by time and distance.

The door opened behind him and he zipped up the bag. He turned to see Laurel slip inside. Her expression was unreadable. His heart ached as he saw the answer in her eyes. "How did it go?"

She shrugged. "As expected. He's not going to give me my trust fund, so I'm leaving. I'm going to get on with my life."

"Are you sure?" Sean asked. "Maybe you should give him a little more time."

"Nope." She walked over to the closet and grabbed the suitcases she'd begun to pack just a day ago. "I'm fine with this. I have a little money in a savings account and I might be able to pick up a teaching job. I need to find an apartment, but until then, I have a few friends I taught with who'll put me up. I'll see if I can stay with Nan Salinger. You met her at my wedding. She was my maid of honor."

"You can stay with me," Sean suggested. "I have a big apartment." He didn't expect her to say yes, but he said a short prayer anyway. He couldn't bear the thought of passing an entire day and night without seeing her or touching her. An ache had settled into his heart and he knew it came from the spot that she was about to abandon.

"Thanks for the offer," Laurel said. "But I need to do this on my own. It's time for me to stand up for myself and stop depending on others. I've had a pretty cushy life, but that's over now."

"What about the center?"

"I don't know. I'm going to try to make it work without my trust fund, but it's going to be tough. Life looked a lot easier when I had five million to throw around. I'll call Amy and tell her that my situation has changed."

"And Rafe's people are still working on the plans and estimates."

"Maybe you should call and tell them to stop," Laurel murmured.

Sean stuffed a stray pair of jeans into his bag. "No. Damn it, Laurel, the center is a good idea. Go ahead and do your presentation to the foundation. Make it work. What do you have to lose?"

"You should be glad this is over," Laurel commented. "Now your life can get back to normal."

"I was beginning to feel like this was normal."

She shook her head. "No. This was just make-believe, Sean. Like magic. We snap our fingers and it's gone."

Sean reached out and took her hand, twisting his fingers around hers. "It wasn't all make-believe. And it's not going to disappear so easily."

He wanted to kiss her, to drag her into his arms and convince himself that nothing had changed between them, that Laurel still wanted him as much as he wanted her. But if their relationship did end here and now, kissing her would only make that end much harder to bear.

"Maybe not," she said with a weak smile. Laurel picked up her purse from where she'd thrown it on the floor, then pulled out her checkbook. "I guess I'd better pay you."

"I don't want your money," Sean said, his anger flaring. Was this so easy for her? To just push him out of her life without a second thought? He'd thought they'd made a connection, something stronger than could be broken with just a shrug and a check.

"I want to. I'm afraid I don't have enough for the whole month. I was expecting a windfall and that didn't come through."

"I wasn't here for a month. Let's just call it even."

"But we had an agreement," she argued. "I can give you two thousand now. Once I get settled and get back to work, I can give you more."

Sean reached in his pocket and withdrew his wallet. He found Laurel's original check inside and handed it to her.

"What's this?"

"I want to make a donation," he said. "To the Louise Carpenter Rand Center for the Arts. Keep your money. Just send me a receipt when you get up and running so I can deduct this on my taxes," he said with a wink.

Laurel stared down at the check, her lower lip trembling. When she looked back up at him again, her eyes had filled with tears. "I'm going to miss you, Sean Quinn."

Sean slipped his hand over her nape and pulled her close, kissing her softly. To hell with his resolve. If this was the last time, then he wanted one good memory to carry with him. "We had a pretty good marriage."

She smiled through her tears. "It was good. Maybe it was so good because we weren't really married."

He gently stroked her cheek, trying to memorize the feel of her skin. "If you need anything at all, I want you to call me, Laurel." He pulled his wallet from his pocket and withdrew a business card.

"That has my phone and cell phone number and you can always reach me at the pub. They'll know where I am."

"I'll remember that."

He wanted to tell her right then, to wrap his arms around her and to murmur the words, to beg her to make a life with him. But Laurel was right. They'd lived in a fantasy world this whole time, a place where they only had to think about eating and sleeping and making love. The honeymoon was over and Sean couldn't be sure that what they'd shared would last.

His brain screamed at him to take the risk, to surrender his soul. But instinct held him back. "I should go," he murmured, knowing that if he stayed a minute longer he might be lost.

Laurel reached up and slipped her arms around his neck, giving him a hug. "I guess I'll be seeing you."

"Not if I see you first," Sean teased. He hoisted his bag over his shoulder and walked to the door. He didn't look back, certain he'd forget all his resolve and find an excuse to stay.

As he walked down the stairs, he saw Alistair waiting at the bottom. He stopped, held out his hand, and the butler shook it. "Thanks for everything, Alistair. You know your beer and you make a helluva breakfast."

"Thank you, Mr. Sean."

"It's just Sean." He glanced up the stairs. "Keep an eye on her, all right?"

"That should be your job," the butler said.

Sean shook his head. "I wish it was, but I'm not sure I'm the guy to do it."

"I think you're the only guy to do it, sir."

Sean clapped the butler on the shoulder, then strode to the door. He considered making a stop in the library to give Sinclair Rand a piece of his mind. But in the end he walked out, walked away from the Mighty Quinn curse, away from the woman who was supposed to be his destiny. Sean wasn't sure if he'd just made the biggest mistake of his life or had saved himself a broken heart. But he figured he'd know soon enough.

9

"As you can see by this map, the location for the Louise Carpenter Rand Center for the Arts is two blocks off Dorchester Avenue and within easy walking distance of two bus lines. Within a ten-block radius, census figures show nearly one thousand school-age children who would benefit from our programs. Working parents would know that their children are safe after school and they'd be assured that their children were participating in an enriching variety of artistic endeavors including dance, music, theater and the visual arts." Laurel pointed nervously to the map, then gave a tremulous smile. "How was that?"

Alistair clapped excitedly. "Oh, very good. I must say I was quite impressed, Miss Laurel."

"I should have pointed to the map when I was talking about the location. I have to remember that."

"No, I thought that was fine. It emphasized your information about the location at the very end."

Laurel had put her final presentation together last night and had brought everything over to the house to show Alistair when she stopped by to pick up more of her clothes. The butler had offered to serve as a practice audience and she'd been grateful for the input. Her displays and charts and floor plans were propped up around the dining room, some on the floor and some on easels that she'd brought along.

"I get so flustered with all the facts and figures," Laurel said. "But I know they're important. Amy says her board of directors likes facts and figures. I have all of it in the handout, but I think they'll want to hear it from me."

"What time is the presentation tomorrow morning?"

"Ten o'clock at the foundation office," she said. "In their boardroom. Amy showed me. There'll be at least ten people there, maybe as many as fifteen." Laurel fussed with the papers she'd laid out on the dining room table. "Would you come? For moral support?"

"Of course I will," Alistair said. He reached into his jacket pocket and withdrew an envelope, holding it out to her.

"What's this?"

"I wanted to be the first to make a donation," he said.

"Oh, you don't have to make—"

"No," Alistair interrupted. "If you're going to make a success of this, you have to learn to accept every donation graciously."

Laurel smiled and plucked the envelope out of his hand. "Thank you very much. Your donation will be put to good use." She opened the envelope and looked at the check inside. Her eyes went wide. "Thirty thousand dollars?"

"Your uncle has paid me very well over the years," Alistair explained. "And I've been lucky with my investments. I can't think of a better cause than this."

Laurel hurried over to him and wrapped her arms around his neck, giving him a fierce hug. "Thank you."

He patted her back. "Now, why don't you come to the kitchen and I'll fix you a sandwich. You've been working so hard, you probably haven't eaten anything all morning."

"I am a little hungry."

She slipped her arm through Alistair's and walked with him through the butler's pantry to the kitchen. After pulling up a stool, Laurel sat at the kitchen worktable. "Thanks for letting me come over and practice in front of you. I really appreciate your input."

"How's the hunt for an apartment going?"

Laurel shrugged. "I'm still sleeping on Nan's sofa."

"And have you seen Sean lately?"

Her stomach did a little somersault at the mention of his name. Sean Quinn. She'd thought about him at least a hundred times a day since they'd parted a month ago. She'd even driven past the pub three or four times, hoping that she'd find the courage to stop in for a bowl of soup and a chance to see him. "We haven't talked."

"Why not? You have two men in your life who love you, Laurel. And you're not talking to either one of them."

"Sinclair doesn't love me." She let the sentence hang in the air, her thought unfinished. She wasn't really sure how Sean felt.

"I think Sinclair misses you. He regrets what happened."

"It's his fault," Laurel said.

Alistair cleared his throat. "No...actually, it's my fault."

"Your fault?"

He set down the jar of mayonnaise that he'd re-trieved from the refrigerator and met her questioning gaze. "While I was in New York with your uncle, I let it slip that you and Sean weren't really husband and wife."

"Alistair! Why would you do that?"

"I wanted to prove to your uncle how far you were willing to go to secure your happiness and to get your trust fund. I thought he needed to know what he was putting you through. And I also convinced him of the fact that you were in love with Sean Quinn."

"Why would you do that?"

"Because I thought you were in love with Sean Quinn."

Laurel sighed. "I was. I am." She moaned softly. "Oh, God, I do love him."

"Imagine my surprise when your uncle told me he thought Sean would make a good husband for you. So the two of us hatched a little plan. We decided to find a way to keep you two together until you both realized how you felt."

Confusion muddled her brain as she tried to under-stand what Alistair was saying. "And...and everything that happened that night was part of your plan?"

"We didn't expect you to get angry and walk out. Sinclair was crushed. He thought he was doing the right thing and it only served to drive you away. I tried to convince him to call you, but he's so stubborn. The apple doesn't fall far from the tree."

Laurel braced her elbows on the table and cupped her chin in her palms. "I can't believe this."

"We managed to make a real mess of it. And I'm sorry for being the source of it all. But you have to know, we only wanted your happiness."

As Laurel considered all that Alistair had revealed, she tried to make sense of what her uncle had done. Why hadn't he just come out and told her how he felt? Why did he constantly have to manipulate her? Was that the only way he knew how to show his love?

"Now, about Sean..." Alistair prompted.

"I think he cares about me. But I don't think his feelings run as deep. It's so hard to tell with him. He keeps so much hidden. He has trouble trusting, and even if he did love me I think he'd deny it for fear that he might get hurt."

Alistair put the ham sandwich he'd made on a plate and handed it to her. "You know him pretty well, don't you?"

"Sometimes I think I do. And other times, I think there's a whole lot more behind that handsome face that I don't understand."

"And you haven't wanted to see him since the two of you left here last month?"

"I figured if he really cared, he'd find me."

"Maybe he figures the same," Alistair suggested.

Laurel slid off the stool and picked up her plate. "I need to get back to work."

Whenever she found herself dwelling on what might have been, she went back to work, focusing her thoughts on the children's center and on her presentation. She shook her head and tried to clear her mind, but talking about Sean hadn't done her any good.

Questions that she'd put aside rushed back into her head.

Laurel wandered into the dining room, then stopped short. Sinclair stood in front of one of the easels, staring at a huge photo of Laurel's mother she had brought along. Laurel had decided to use the photo in the presentation to put a face to her dreams, to make it clear why she'd had the dream in the first place.

"You loved her, didn't you?" she said.

Sinclair's shoulders stiffened and he slowly turned to face her, his ivory-handled cane clutched in his hand. His eyes were wistful and his face showed nothing of the hard expression it usually wore. "She didn't love me."

Laurel slowly crossed the room. "That must have been so difficult for you. To live in this house with her and my father. To see their happiness every day."

He shook his head. "No. I considered myself lucky to be able to look at her beautiful face every morning and every evening. And after she died, I was reminded of her when I looked at you. You look very much like her." His eyes misted over for a moment and Sinclair turned away, focusing his attention on the other easels she'd set up along one side of the room.

"This seems like a very ambitious plan," he said, walking down the line of charts and photos.

"It is," Laurel replied. "I'm doing my presentation for the Aldrich-Sloane Family Foundation tomorrow morning. I'm hoping that they'll decide to fund the project."

Sinclair was silent for a long time. "You've grown up," he murmured.

"I'm twenty-six years old," Laurel said. "I know what I want to do with my life."

"And you don't let anything stand in your way to get it, do you? Not even a foolish old man."

Laurel reached out and placed her hand on his arm. "You're not a foolish old man," she said. "You just know what you want and you don't let anything stand in your way. We're alike in that way. It must be a Rand family trait."

"Can you forgive an old man for his selfishness?"

Her gaze met his and for the first time in her life she saw how much he cared about her. Sinclair was family and the least she could give him was her forgiveness—and her love. "I can."

He nodded, patting her hand as he did. "Good. And I think I can admit that I was wrong about your trust fund. This is a fine use of your inheritance. In fact, it might do me some good to put a little of my own money into this project."

Laurel couldn't believe what she'd just heard. "You're going to give me my trust fund?"

"I'll have the bank transfer it to your name in the morning. You'll have to sign some papers, but that shouldn't take long."

Tears flooded Laurel's eyes and she grabbed her uncle and gave him a quick hug. He sputtered slightly, surprised at her show of affection, then reached out and patted her shoulder. "There is one thing I'd like you to consider. Two things, actually."

Laurel's breath caught in her throat. Was he about to lay down another condition? "What is that?"

"First, I'd like for you to move back into the house.

It's your house and you belong here. I'm going back to Maine soon. And, second, I'd like you to go find that young man of yours. I enjoy him. He doesn't take any crap from a rich old man. And I've got some new coins I want to show him."

"No more conditions?" Laurel asked.

"No more conditions," Sinclair agreed.

They strolled out into the foyer and Laurel walked with him to the library. "When I was younger, I fancied myself quite the painter," Sinclair commented as he settled himself into his huge wing chair.

"Really? A painter?"

"I was quite good, but my parents insisted that I take up something more practical. An artist couldn't make a good living unless he had a great talent."

"Maybe you should take up painting again," Laurel suggested. "You have the time and we could go out and buy some paint and brushes. It's not too late. It's never too late to make your dreams come true, Uncle."

"No, I suppose it isn't," Sinclair said.

As Laurel sat in the library, sharing a brandy with her uncle, her thoughts drifted to dreams of another kind. Every night since Sean had left, he'd come to her in her sleep, a strong, certain presence that she found herself longing for in the morning when she awoke.

Now that all her other dreams were falling into place, maybe it was time to make one last dream come true.

SEAN STARED at the office door, then reached out and ran his hand over the block letters painted on the window. "Quinn Private Investigations," he murmured.

He'd found the small office space in Southie last month. The building was on a main thoroughfare and his second-floor office had a window that also boasted the name of his new business, a nice way to advertise that he'd moved in.

Sean hadn't expect to rent the office so quickly. Though his savings had barely covered the first three months' rent, he hadn't let that stop him as it had in the past. He'd learned an important lesson from Laurel. Waiting until the perfect moment for your dreams to come true was a waste of precious time.

He and Laurel were so different. She met life head-on and fearlessly, unafraid of making mistakes. And he'd always been so careful, so measured and wary. She'd shown him how to go out and take a gamble, accept the risks and just jump off that cliff. There would never be the perfect time to start building the life he wanted, so why not start right away?

Sean sat at the desk he'd salvaged from the basement of Olivia's antique store and kicked up his feet. He'd already found one new client, a small armored-car company that needed independent background checks done on its employees. And he'd had a few walk-in clients since he'd opened his doors, two deadbeat dads to track down and a runaway daughter.

But there was one part of his life that he hadn't quite squared away yet. He sucked in a deep breath and let it out slowly. Laurel. He knew from Amy that her grant had been approved and that she'd purchased the building in Dorchester. He also knew that she'd moved back to the mansion. But all his information was secondhand or hearsay. He hadn't talked to Laurel since the day he'd walked out of the house in Cohasset.

The first week after his "marriage" had ended, Sean was sure he'd done the right thing. Though he'd spent all of his idle time thinking about her, he'd hoped those thoughts would gradually fade. But when they hadn't by the third week, he began to realize that maybe they never would. Hell, if this wasn't love, he didn't know what was.

A soft knock sounded on his office door and he swung his feet off the desk and stood. When he pulled the door open, his mother stood on the other side, a huge plant in her arms.

"Ma," he said, grabbing the plant. "What are you doing here?"

"I brought you an office-warming gift. A plant always brightens up any decor."

"How did you know where to find the place?"

"It's all everyone's been talking about at the pub. Your da's been passing out your business cards like free beer on St. Paddy's Day."

Sean grabbed a stack of newspapers from the seat of an old wooden chair and dusted it off with his hand. "Have a seat."

Fiona smiled, pleased by the offer. "This is a nice office. Lots of light." She glanced around. "When your da and I first moved to Southie, there used to be an accountant's office here." She shook her head. "That was a lifetime ago. So, this is a big step, isn't it? Your own office."

Sean nodded and sat. "I have stationery, too. When I do my reports they'll look really official. And look at that." He pointed over his shoulder. "I've got a fax machine and a computer. I bought the fax secondhand from Rafe, and Brian gave me his old computer. I'm even thinking about getting a Web site. And when I have enough money, maybe a secretary."

"You've got everything you need," Fiona said.

"Yeah." Sean paused. "Well, not everything."

A long silence grew between them, Fiona fussing with a loose button on her sweater and Sean tapping a pen on his desk.

"What happened with Laurel?" she finally asked.

Sean shrugged. A month ago he could barely stand to be in the same room with his mother and now he felt comfortable enough to confide in her. Jeez, it was hard to believe he was the same guy. "I don't know. It just ended—as quickly as it began. No reason. Or maybe we just didn't have a reason to keep it going."

"Did you argue?"

"No, we just walked away. Maybe if we'd had a few more weeks together something might have happened. But we were barely together for a week. People don't fall in love that fast."

"Your father and I did," Fiona said. "The instant I saw him I knew I'd marry him. He felt the same way. That happened a lot in Seamus's family."

"And look at what hap—" Sean snapped his mouth shut. "Sorry. I didn't mean to—"

"No," Fiona said. "You're right. Sometimes love at first sight doesn't work out." A slow smile curled her lips. "Oh, but sometimes it does. We never know until we try."

"I don't want to make a mistake. I don't want to

spend my life like Da, bitter and angry, full of resentment."

"Your father and I let that happen to us," Fiona insisted. "We were both too stubborn to admit our marriage was in trouble. He didn't want to face his failures and I refused to believe I couldn't help him. Sometimes I wonder if we'd just sat down back then and talked to each other, really talked, whether things might have been different. Can you talk to this girl, Laurel?"

"I can talk to her like I've never talked to anyone. Even Brian. I can say anything to her—except maybe how much I love her."

"You love her," Fiona said.

"I do."

"Then why are you sitting here in this office telling me?"

Sean smiled ruefully. "Maybe when I figure that one out, I'll know what to do." He furrowed his hands in his hair, pressing his palms against his temples. "I should go see her."

"I think that would be best," Fiona said.

"Now?"

"Why not? There's no time like the present."

Sean pushed up from his chair and paced back and forth across the width of the tiny office. "All right. I'm gonna do it. I'm gonna tell her. And if she doesn't love me, then I'll deal with it." He hurried to the door, then stopped and walked back to his mother. "Thanks."

"You're welcome," she said.

Just as he got to the door, Fiona called his name. "Wait, I nearly forgot the reason I came," she said. "Two weeks from Saturday we're having a family get-together at Keely's house. About five in the evening. She and Rafe are all moved in and they'd like everyone to be there." Fiona met his gaze. "*I'd* like everyone to be there. I know you usually don't attend family functions, but this is—"

"I'll be there," Sean said, anxious to leave.

"You will? Do you promise?"

He nodded. "I promise."

"You can bring Laurel," she said.

Sean nodded, impatient to get going. "We'll see. Could you write the date in my book there, on the desk? And lock the door as you leave."

His car was parked half a block away. By the time he pulled out into traffic, he'd decided to try Dorchester first. Amy had told him that work had begun on Laurel's building and she'd been consumed with the details. If he got lucky, he'd find her there. He considered calling first, but the element of surprise would work to his advantage. If she wasn't in Dorchester he'd head out to the mansion in Cohasset.

As he drove, Sean practiced what he was going to say, knowing he'd probably only have one chance to get it right. This was the single most important moment in his life and he didn't want to mumble and bumble his way through it. "I love you," he murmured. "Laurel, I love you. I love you more than..." He cursed softly. "No, just keep it simple."

But what if she questioned his declaration? What if she asked him why he loved her? God, he wished he had Brendan along—or Brian. They'd always been so good with words. They'd be able to tell him exactly what to say to make her believe him. Sean reached into his jacket pocket for his cell phone, then thought better of the idea and tossed the phone onto the seat beside him.

"Why do I love her?" He took a deep breath. "One. I love her because she's the strongest person I've ever known. Two. Because she can see inside my soul. Three. Because when she looks at me, I feel like the luckiest guy in the world."

Sean groaned. "God, that sounds so hokey. Why do I love you, Laurel? Because when I'm with you, my life suddenly makes sense?"

He turned south toward Dorchester, weaving in and out of traffic. When he was just a few blocks from Laurel's building he pulled to the curb and took a moment to organize his thoughts. But a million words rattled around in his head and he couldn't seem to put them in any decent order.

Maybe if he had paid more attention in school he could have quoted poetry or recited a few lines from Shakespeare, but "Romeo, Romeo, wherefore art thou Romeo" and "To be or not to be" didn't really apply. He'd always been a man of very few words and "I love you, Laurel" was what best expressed his thoughts.

By the time he pulled up to the old storefront he'd decided simplicity would serve him best. His stomach tensed when he saw Laurel's car parked out front. As he walked to the front door he fought off a flood of nausea. "I love you, Laurel. I love you."

The door was unlocked and as he walked through the open space on the first floor the voices of construction workers and the sounds of power tools filled the air. He approached a guy holding a T square. "Hey there. I'm looking for Laurel Rand."

"She's upstairs."

Sean nodded. "Thanks." He took the stairs two at a time, anxious now to see her. It had seemed like months, years even, since he'd looked into her eyes, and he wondered if he really remembered how beautiful she was. When he got to the top of the stairs Sean stopped. Laurel stood in the cavernous room, her back to him, her face tipped up.

He watched her for a long time from the shadows of the stairwell door, watched as she slowly turned, then did a little ballet step. She held her arms above her head, went up on her toes and did three neat pirouettes. But she froze in the middle of the fourth when she saw him step into the room. Her eyes grew wide and she plopped back down on her heels.

She smoothed her hands over the front of her faded jeans. "Sean."

He took another step into the room and opened his mouth, ready to profess his love. But all that came out was her name. "Laurel," he murmured. God, she was beautiful. He'd forgotten how pale her hair was and how it curled around her face. He'd forgotten the exact color of her eyes and the perfect shape of her mouth.

"What are you doing here?" she asked.

"I came to see you. I have something I have to tell you." He swallowed hard. "How are you?"

"I'm fine."

Sean nodded. "Good. Good. You look fine. You look better than fine." He glanced around. "And the place is looking fine, too."

She smiled, confusion coloring her expression. "Everything is fine."

Hell, this was not going well. He couldn't seem to make small talk, yet he couldn't just blurt out what he'd come to say. Then an idea popped into his head. He'd go back to where it all started. "I came here because I wanted to talk to you about a problem I have."

She moved toward him. "Are you all right?"

"I'm fine. It's just this problem. You see, I'm in need of a...a wife. I had this one woman and we got along great. But I was a real dope and I blew it. I didn't tell her how I felt. I should have, but I was afraid she might not feel the same way about me."

"Maybe she did," Laurel murmured, her gaze fixed on his, her eyes piercing the depths of his soul.

"Maybe. Anyway, I have this proposition for you." He reached into his pocket and grabbed his wallet. "I have seven...twelve...fourteen dollars here and—" he shoved his hand into the front pocket of his jeans "—and seventy-nine cents." Sean held the money out to her in the palm of his hand. "How many days will this buy me?"

"Are you asking me to be your wife again?" Her voice trembled and her gaze darted over his features, as if she was trying to see the truth there.

"I am," he said. "And I'm willing to pay you $14.79 if you say yes. But this time I don't want it to be pretend. I want to marry you for real, Laurel. I want to make a life with you."

Laurel's smile grew wider. "Are you sure?"

"I'm sure I love you, Laurel. I'm sure I never expected to need you so much. And I'm sure I want to spend the rest of my life with you."

"We haven't known each other for very long."

"I know all I need to know."

Laurel reached out and hesitantly took the money from his hand. "This is all you have to give me?"

"I have my heart and my soul, and I have my devotion to give you. And a promise that I'll make you happy." Sean reached into his pocket again and pulled out one last dime. "And I have ten cents more."

Laurel laughed softly. "Ten cents. Well, that makes a big difference. For $14.79, I would have given you five or six years. But for $14.89, you can have the rest of my life."

Sean took one last step toward her and Laurel threw herself into his arms, the money falling to the floor, their mouths meeting in a frantic kiss. The taste of her was like a drug, soothing his nerves, exciting his desire. His hands moved to her face, skimming over her features as if he had to prove to himself that this really was Laurel in his arms.

"Say it again," he murmured. "Say you want to marry me."

"I do," Laurel said, laughing. "I do, I do, I do."

"I promise to make you happy, Laurel. And I promise I'll never walk away again." He grabbed her waist and lifted her feet off the floor. "I love Laurel Rand," he shouted, his words echoing in the huge room.

"And I love Sean Quinn," she replied. She hugged him. "That really isn't so hard to say, is it?"

Sean shook his head. "I love you, Laurel." As he kissed her again, a wave of emotion washed over him.

Love wasn't a curse and it wasn't an affliction. Instead, it was a power, deeper than anything he'd ever known in his life. And it was also the one thing that connected him with all his Mighty Quinn ancestors. For despite his father's cautionary tales, it had been and always would be a woman who made the Quinns the mightiest men of all.

Epilogue

THE TINY GARDEN behind Keely and Rafe's house was strung with white lights that glittered in the dark October night. Sean stared down from a second-floor bedroom at the small group gathered outside. Conor and Dylan were waiting with their wives, Olivia and Meggie, and Olivia held Riley, the first Quinn grandchild. Nearby, Brendan scanned a table laid out with food while Amy fussed with a flower arrangement in the center. The rest of the family was running around the house, getting ready for the wedding ceremony that was scheduled to start in just ten minutes.

Sean turned back to the mirror and tried once again to tie the black bow tie. This time he managed to get both sides to come out even, though a bit tilted. Rafe poked his head in the door. "Are you almost ready?"

Sean nodded, then raked his fingers through his hair. "Yep, I'm ready to go. Have you seen Laurel?"

"She's downstairs waiting for you."

"Is everyone else ready to go?"

Rafe nodded. Sean gave his tie one last tug, then followed his brother-in-law down the stairs and into the rear of the house. He found Laurel waiting in the kitchen with Brian and Lily. The moment she saw him, she smiled.

"You look so handsome," she said.

Sean leaned close and brushed a kiss across her lips. "I had trouble with the tie."

"It looks perfect."

He smoothed his hands around her waist, so tiny above the wide skirt of her gown. The wedding had been billed as a formal event, though invitations had been sent only a few days before. He'd had to rush to rent a tux and get it fitted. Everyone in the family had believed that the evening was a simple family get-together to celebrate Keely and Rafe's new house. But the surprise had delighted them all.

"How is Da doing?" Brian asked, peering through the French doors that led to the garden.

"Your father looks a little nervous," Laurel said. "I think he would have been happier if the wedding had been held at the pub."

Sean gave her waist a squeeze. "I never thought this would happen. Da and Ma getting married again. But it feels right."

"I think it's sweet," she said. "And so romantic."

"Technically, they're already married. They never got a divorce."

Laurel reached up and brushed his hair off his forehead. "After all that time apart they realized they still loved each other. That's pretty amazing."

"It's not hard to imagine," Sean said. "I plan to love you for the rest of my life. And no time apart, not a day, or a month, or a year is going to change how I feel about you."

"One of these days, we're going to have to plan our wedding," she said.

"I'm not going to wear a tux," he said immediately.

Then he shrugged. "I guess I could wear a tux if you want me to."

"Maybe we shouldn't have a big wedding. We could take the whole family up to Deer Island and get married at my uncle's house. It's beautiful around the holidays with the snow and the pines. And I know he would love it if we got married there."

"Just send me the invitation and I'll be there. I'll marry you anytime and anywhere you want me to. Unlike your last wedding, you won't need to hire a groom."

"We should really thank Eddie," she said smiling fondly. "The poor guy practically introduced us, and all he'll have to show for it is a prison record."

"Here's to Eddie," Sean responded and kissed her cheek.

Keely hurried into the room. "All right," she said breathlessly. "We're ready to start. Everyone get settled outside. Ma is about to come down. All the brothers need to stand behind Seamus. And make a nice straight line for the photos. And don't forget to smile."

"Come on," Sean said, taking Laurel's hand and tucking it into the crook of his arm. "I'll walk you down the aisle."

They walked out into the garden and Laurel stood next to Lily, Brian's fiancée. As Sean took his place with his brothers, he let his gaze wander over the family that had gathered in the garden. There had been a time when he'd felt like an outsider, like he didn't belong to the family he'd been born into. But now, as he gazed at the woman he loved, he realized just what Laurel had given him.

He remembered his mother's words as Fiona walked through the garden to join Sean's father in front of the priest. She'd claimed that all the Quinns had a bit of magic in their blood, carried with them from Ireland. There had been a time when it would have taken every fairy and gnome and wizard on the Emerald Isle to make Sean Quinn believe in love.

But all it had really taken was one woman—Laurel Rand. The woman he'd been destined to meet all along, the woman who had worked her own magic on his heart. And the woman he'd marry and love for the rest of his life.

And as for the Quinn family curse, in fact, it had been a blessing. Something so wondrous that, by future generations, it might be told as another legend of the Mighty Quinns, a tale of how love had captured six brothers, one by one, and shown them what had been in their hearts all along.

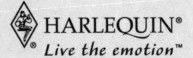
HTSLIH

If you enjoyed what you just read,
then we've got an offer you can't resist!

Take 2 bestselling love stories FREE!

Plus get a FREE surprise gift!

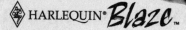

HARLEQUIN® Blaze™

In September 2003

Look for the latest sizzling sensation from
USA TODAY bestselling author

Suzanne Forster

BRIEF ENCOUNTERS

When Swan McKenna's accused of stealing five million dollars from her racy men's underwear company, Brief Encounters, a federal agent moves in on the place and on her. With his government-issue good looks, little does Swan expect by-the-book Rob Gaines to help her out by reluctantly agreeing to strut his stuff in her upcoming fashion show. Nor does she realize that once she sees Rob in his underwear, she won't be able to resist catching him out of it....

And that their encounters will be anything but brief!

*Don't miss this superspecial Blaze™ volume #101
at your favorite local retailer.*

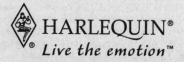

HARLEQUIN®
Live the emotion™

Visit us at www.tryblaze.com

HBSFBE

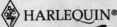